THE LYTTLETON CASE

'THE DETECTIVE STORY CLUB is a clearing house for the best detective and mystery stories chosen for you by a select committee of experts. Only the most ingenious crime stories will be published under the THE DETECTIVE STORY CLUB imprint. A special distinguishing stamp appears on the wrapper and title page of every THE DETECTIVE STORY CLUB book—the Man with the Gun. Always look for the Man with the Gun when buying a Crime book.'

Wm. Collins Sons & Co. Ltd., 1929

Now the Man with the Gun is back in this series of COLLINS CRIME CLUB reprints, and with him the chance to experience the classic books that influenced the Golden Age of crime fiction.

D1356110

THE DETECTIVE STORY CLUB

FURTHER TITLES IN PREPARATION

THE LYTTLETON CASE

A STORY OF CRIME

BY

R. A. V. MORRIS

WITH AN INTRODUCTION BY
DOUGLAS A. ANDERSON

COLLINS
CRIME
CLUB

COLLINS CRIME CLUB
An imprint of HarperCollins*Publishers*
1 London Bridge Street
London SE1 9GF
www.harpercollins.co.uk

This edition 2017

First published in Great Britain by
W. Collins Sons & Co. Ltd 1922
Published by The Detective Story Club Ltd 1930

Introduction © Douglas A. Anderson 2017

A catalogue record for this book is available from the British Library

ISBN 978-0-00-821624-5

Typeset in Bulmer MT Std by
Palimpsest Book Production Ltd, Falkirk, Stirlingshire
Printed and bound in Great Britain by
Clays Ltd, St Ives plc

MIX
Paper from
responsible sources
FSC
www.fsc.org   FSC™ C007454

INTRODUCTION

For a first novel by an unknown author, *The Lyttleton Case* by R.A.V. Morris fared pretty well. Published by W. Collins Sons of London in April 1922, it was reprinted a month afterwards, with third and fourth impressions in 1923, and a fifth in 1926. A cheap two shilling edition appeared in April 1927. And the Detective Club published a new popular edition at 6d in February 1930. But Morris published no follow-up books, and thereafter *The Lyttleton Case* lapsed into obscurity. It was recalled by Jacques Barzun and Wendell Hertig Taylor in their *Catalogue of Crime* (1971; revised 1989) as 'an early specimen of the well-written, slow, carefully plotted puzzle . . . this is an acceptable tale of murder, impersonation, and abduction, with entertaining asides about the contemporary scene'.

The author's full name was Ronald Arthur Vennor Morris. He was one of seven children (three of whom died in infancy) of Alfred Arthur Vennor Morris (1849–1884), one of a family of chemical manufacturers in Carmarthenshire, Wales, and Rosa Leach (1845–1883), who came from a very large family that lived in Devizes Castle in Wiltshire. Ronald was the oldest surviving child—he was born at Wernoleu, one of three family houses on the slopes of Bettws Mountain near Ammanford, on 19 September 1877. His sole younger brother was Kenneth Morris (1879–1937), whose writings are seminal in the field of fantasy. These include two works expanding upon the Welsh *Mabinogion*, *The Fates of the Princes of Dyfed* (1914) and its sequel *Book of the Three Dragons* (1930; expanded to include its unpublished ending in 2005); *The Secret Mountain and Other Tales* (1926); the posthumous fantasy of the Toltecs of ancient Mexico, *The Chalchuihite Dragon* (1992); and *The Dragon Path: Collected Tales of Kenneth Morris* (1995), edited by Douglas A. Anderson.

Rosa Morris died on 7 September 1883, seemingly as a result of a difficult pregnancy, which resulted also in the death of one of twin girls born about ten days earlier. Alfred died on 1 August 1884, and the four surviving Morris children were thus orphaned. New laws regulating trade had also caused a failure of the family business. Ronald, Kenneth and their two younger sisters were sent first to their mother's family at Devizes Castle, and then on to London, where the boys were sent to school at Christ's Hospital, then located in the centre of London. Christ's Hospital was a traditional English school, and because the boys there wore long blue coats (with yellow stockings) it was known as the Bluecoat School. Ronald left the school in 1893 at the age-limit of sixteen; Kenneth left in 1895.

Ronald apparently went into business, working in London, after leaving Christ's Hospital. Both he and Kenneth joined Theosophical Societies, but they joined different sects. Ronald joined that run by Annie Besant out of Adyar, India, while Kenneth joined the Katherine Tingley branch, and later moved to its headquarters in southern California for twenty-two years (1908–1930). In 1898 Ronald married Eliza Augusta Jevons (1858–1945), the daughter of a solicitor who was nineteen years his senior. They had one daughter, Eileen Mary Vennor Morris (1900–1972). Both Ronald and Eliza Morris were active in the Theosophical Society and in the Order of the Golden Dawn occult society. Ronald seems to have worked for a while as a merchant and later at a bank. He and his family lived in London through at least the 1910s, but by 1930 they had settled in Hove. When Kenneth returned to England in 1930, he spent some time with his brother before settling in Wales.

Ronald contributed occasional articles and poems to theosophical publications, but *The Lyttleton Case* is apparently his only work of fiction. The competitive nature of the relationship between the brothers suggests that Ronald might have attempted fiction because Kenneth had done so.

The Lyttleton Case begins with the disappearance of James Lyttleton. His daughter Doris and her fiancé, Basil Dawson, a newspaperman on the staff of the *Daily Gazette*, come to study the mystery, and in the meantime Chief Inspector James Candlish engages upon an unrelated investigation. Gradually the threads of each story come together to meet in resolution.

Morris's familiarity with the detective fiction genre is exemplified in the jovial thoughts of Police Constable Higginson in Chapter XII, who 'was a diligent reader of detective fiction, and sometimes, over his last pipe before going to bed, he allowed his mind to form alluring pictures of the day when the name of Higginson would be as famous as that of Lecocq [sic] himself. In the meantime, when on night duty, he compared himself with C. Auguste Dupin.' Dupin was the invention of Edgar Allan Poe (1809–1849), and it was with his first appearance in 'The Murders in the Rue Morgue' (1841) that the detective fiction story was inaugurated. Monsieur Lecoq was the detective in a series of books by the French writer Émile Gaboriau (1832–1873), whose works were very popular in English translations in the 1870s, and Lecoq was a major influence on Arthur Conan Doyle's stories of Sherlock Holmes, who became the world's most popular fictional detective.

Police Constable Higginson also makes inevitable references to Sherlock Holmes, and mentions a book more contemporary to the time of writing, *The Cask* (1920), the first detective novel by Freeman Wills Crofts (1879–1957).

The Times Literary Supplement called *The Lyttleton Case* 'a complicated detective story, which might have contained more exciting incidents' (20 April 1922). The *Sheffield Daily Independent* called it a 'cleverly constructed crime story, with the dramatic situations well sustained' (12 April 1922), while the *Aberdeen Daily Journal* found fault with its 'somewhat heavy-handed jocularity' and felt that 'the action of the tale is impeded by an excess of padding' (6 April 1922).

R.A.V. Morris died of prostate cancer, at the age of 66, at a nursing home in Brighton, on 30 November 1943. According to his death certificate he was a 'retired Company Director'. It is a pity that he published no further cases of Chief Inspector James Candlish. *The Lyttleton Case* certainly feels that it should be part of a series of novels, but we are left to accept it as a promising one-off by one of the few detective story writers to come from Wales.

DOUGLAS A. ANDERSON
December 2016

EDITOR'S PREFACE

WHAT do you think of a detective story that runs you down to the banks of a little stream in Surrey to Liverpool and New York and back again; introduces you to a charming heroine; a hero who is a journalist and a poet; a detective who is a naturalist as well as a policeman; a variety of thrills and much not too subtle humour before it makes you begin to believe that you have a sort of idea who really committed the murder? Personally, we think it the sort of tale to make one long for the weekend and pray for the type of weather that makes stopping indoors compulsory.

Mr R. A. V. Morris is certainly to be congratulated on the skill with which he has handled an extremely difficult theme. The situations are novel and they are worked out with rare patience and realism. Mr Morris, moreover, has created three splendid characters in Dawson, a young journalist, Doris Lyttleton, and Inspector Candlish. The last-named is engaged on the Lyttleton case and the author's expert knowledge of the methods of Scotland Yard are emphasised in the inspector's activities. It is a change to have a detective who is not a posing amateur but a prosaic and quite likeable professional from Scotland Yard, and this concession to common sense certainly increases our sense of obligation to Mr Morris.

Above all, the secret is well kept and the reader is left guessing almost to the last page.

THE EDITOR
FROM THE ORIGINAL DETECTIVE STORY CLUB EDITION
February 1930

CHAPTER I

'Every step we take is an adventure into the unknown from which there may be no returning.'

LAMOND'S *Aphorisms*

ON the morning of the 1st of July, 19—, Mr James Lyttleton was breakfasting with his daughter Doris in the pleasant, old-fashioned morning-room of his Hampstead residence. Long Vistas was one of those charming late eighteenth century houses of time-darkened red brick, which, half hidden by high garden walls and the foliage of planes and chestnuts, are so characteristic of the roads bordering on the Heath.

Mr Lyttleton was a widower with one child, a daughter, who kept house for him. He was the senior partner in a large firm of financiers. With his keen gray eyes, his expression, shrewd and alert, yet not unkindly, his well-cut, somewhat aggressive clean-shaven jaw and tight fitting lips, his graying hair and his comfortable figure clothed in the choicest products of Savile Row tailoring, he was a specimen of the best type of those prosperous middle-class Englishmen for whose special delectation this world appears to have been made: the land to produce raw materials for their trade and manufacture; the sea to carry their ships; and the mass of men and women to produce wealth beyond the dreams of a mere Midas or Crœsus. His daughter Doris was less typical and more individualised: she had intellectual and artistic tastes; read Wells and Shaw; was a member of the Fabian Society and the Arts League of Service; with all these eccentricities, however, she could not be regarded as a crank, for she fully appreciated the motor-car, servants, generous dress allowance, and other good things that resulted from her father's activities in the City, however much she might in theory

1

criticise the Stock Exchange and all its works as parasitical on the economic life of the community. For the rest she was distinctly pretty and intelligent looking; her fair hair, which had been 'bobbed' during the war, was now growing again, and her dress suggested an expensive compromise between the rigidly orthodox opinions of her Bond Street dressmaker and the more heterodox taste which rules at the Four Arts' Club, of which she was an active member.

It was Mr Lyttleton's usual custom to spend the half-hour following breakfast over a cigarette and *The Times*; but this morning, after reading with a frown one of the letters in his post, he looked up at his daughter and said, 'I am sorry to say, Doris, that I must be at the office early to attend to some rather tiresome business.'

'That's hard luck, dad,' said she; 'shall I order the car for you?'

'Yes, please, my dear; tell Harrison to be at the front door at a quarter to nine.'

Doris gave the necessary instructions, and when he had finished breakfast her father set off for the City: he said nothing whatever to lead her to expect that he would not return in the evening at his usual time, which was about half-past five. She was therefore somewhat surprised when she got home about half-past six o'clock in the evening, after attending a matinee performance of *Candida*, to find awaiting her a telegram which had been handed in at Euston Station at 5.30 p.m.

'To Liverpool on urgent business, hope return tomorrow.—DAD.'

'He might have 'phoned through before he went, and told me a little more,' thought Doris. 'I am sure he had no idea of going to Liverpool when he left home this morning.'

With this reflection Doris left the subject; and the following morning did no more than wonder in passing, what time her father would get back home. She had made an engagement to meet her fiancé in town for lunch and a visit to the Cubist Exhibition. Just as she was about to leave the house she heard the double rat-tat of a telegraph boy. A telegram was brought in, and to her surprise she read:

'Compelled to go to New York, will wire from there.—DAD.'

She noticed that the message had been handed in at Lime Street Station, Liverpool, at 10.45 a.m.

Now Doris knew that her father had large business interests in the United States, and that he had in the past paid several flying visits to New York; she therefore took the news of his sudden departure almost as a matter of course, although he had never before set off quite as suddenly on so long a journey.

It was his custom, she knew, to keep a kit bag at the office, packed with all the necessaries for a short stay away from home; and he would have no difficulty in buying in Liverpool whatever else he needed for the voyage. She therefore did no more than to ring up Cook's at Ludgate Circus, from whom she ascertained that the *Ruritania* was leaving Liverpool for New York that day, and was due to arrive in the capital of American commerce about midday on the 7th.

Basil Dawson, Doris Lyttleton's fiancé, was a young man of twenty-eight, on the staff of that very enterprising newspaper, the *Daily Gazette*. He was not only a smart journalist, but had begun to win distinction in other and less ephemeral branches of literature. He was one of the few English poets of the younger generation who still believed that poetry is something more than prose cut up arbitrarily into lines of irregular length; and it was whispered with horror among the '*Vers librists*' that he had actually been guilty of writing sonnets. He was tall, dark, wore pince-nez, was a moderate athlete, and avoided, as the devil avoids holy water, all affectations in speech, manner, and appearance. He had not only the imagination of a poet, but he could, unless his feelings were too much stirred, think and act quickly and decisively in practical matters as well—a very strong combination.

Basil and Doris had met each other at a tennis club of which they were both members; and their acquaintance had, under the stimulus of common tastes and interests, rapidly ripened into love. Their engagement had been announced only a few weeks before the opening of this narrative.

So it was that on the 2nd of July, 19— Doris took the Tube from Hampstead Station and found Basil waiting for her in the booking office at Leicester Square. He had been commissioned by his editor to write up the summer exhibition of cubist paintings at the Dover Street Gallery, and he wished not only to enjoy the pleasure of having Doris with him, but he knew that her criticisms of the pictures would be worth listening to, and would be of real help to him in writing his article.

In this world, unfortunately, the requirements of the body must take precedence of those of the mind. Even a Shakespeare must eat before he can write: so it was that for Doris and Basil, lunch had to come before art. Basil suggested the grill room at the Criterion, but Doris said that she wanted a change from what she was accustomed to at home, where the food was invariably well cooked and of the finest quality. When out, she liked something more adventurous, and on the present occasion insisted on taking Basil to the X.Y.Z. café in Piccadilly, where, as she told him, every dish was an experiment, often a surprise. Where half the contents of a cup of coffee was invariably slopped into the saucer; where veal and ham pie was often made of pork; where eggs, ordered poached, arrived at table boiled; where, in fact, one never knew what was coming next, what it was made of, or what one would have to pay for it.

Basil, who had not been brought up in the orderly luxury of Long Vistas, had other ideas of romance, but in those early days of their engagement invariably gave in to Doris. So to the X.Y.Z. café they went; and from there to Dover Street.

By the aid of the catalogue they were able to identify a number of the pictures, and they spent a delightful afternoon, marred only by an argument, which did not quite develop into a quarrel, about one undoubted masterpiece which the catalogue described as 'No. 423—Portrait of a Lady'; both admired it, but Doris maintained that it was hung upside down, while Basil was certain that it had been wrongly ticketed, and was in reality No. 422—'Ruins at Ypres.' However, they made it up afterwards over a cup of tea at Gunter's, and agreed that, at any rate, the colour effects were very fine.

There was no letter from her father when she reached home that evening, so Doris made up her mind to await with patience the arrival of the *Ruritania* at New York, when she would certainly get some news of his movements.

CHAPTER II

'On a seaweed bed he lies
Gazing up with sightless eyes
Through the ripples to the skies.'

DRAKE

CHIEF INSPECTOR JAMES CANDLISH of the Criminal Investigation
Department, Scotland Yard, was a policeman by profession,
and most of his waking hours were necessarily given up to the
routine of his office—supervising the work of his subordinates,
receiving and acting on their reports, and in cases of more than,
usual importance or complexity, himself conducting the necessary inquiries; but his passion was natural history, and every
moment off duty he devoted to exploring the fields, heaths, and
woods round London, for rare plants, butterflies, or birds.

It was his dream that some day he might discover a new
species which would immortalise his name.

It was, however, precisely because his soul was above detection, that he made an unusually good detective, and he pursued
the solution of the tangled cases with which he had to deal,
with almost but not quite the same ardour, insight, and dogged-
ness which he devoted to his search for the golden oriole or a
specimen of one of the rarer ferns.

It is difficult to describe the Inspector's appearance when
on duty, for it was one of his favourite maxims that a detective
should strike a typically average note in person, manner, and
dress; and to this maxim he lived up most successfully. Of
medium height, with brown hair and eyes, an elastic walk and
a quietly brisk manner, he looked less than his age, which was
forty-five; and he appeared so ordinary, so much in tone with
his environment, wherever he happened to be, that no one was

6

tempted to look at him twice, or to take any undue interest in his movements: and this, of course, was precisely the effect he aimed at producing.

A few days before the events recorded in the last chapter, Inspector Candlish had set out for his annual holiday; which he had determined to devote to an exploration of the flora and fauna of the Southshire downs.

He had already spent several delightful days in the pursuit of his hobby when, on the morning of the 6th of July, after an early breakfast, he left his hotel at Low Harbour, to follow inland the course of the little river which joins the sea at that ancient port.

Attired in a tourist suit of homespun, with butterfly net, opera glasses, and collecting box, the Inspector looked less like a policeman than ever as he tramped across the low lying marshes which lay immediately behind the town towards the high rolling downs in the distant background.

The sun was shining brightly, the air was cool and sweet, and there was a tang of the sea in the breeze: in fact, it was one of those almost perfect days that occur sometimes when May has not been left too far behind and August is still far enough in the future.

By noon the Inspector had progressed about four miles inland after a most satisfactory morning's work; so he sat down by the side of the stream to eat his sandwiches, smoke his pipe, and enter up in his pocket-book notes of his natural history observations. He was reclining at ease with pen in hand and pipe in mouth, finishing a short description of the sedge warblers, yellow wagtails, dippers, and kingfishers he had seen during his walk, when his eye was attracted by a glimpse of something white in the stream a little way from where he was. He got up to examine it; and, hardened as his calling made him, could not resist a thrill of horrified surprise to find, resting on and partly hidden by the mud which formed the bed of the stream, the body of a man.

To recover it single handed was beyond his powers; and, as the spot was a lonely one, no help was likely to be forthcoming in the immediate neighbourhood. After a moment's hesitation, therefore, Candlish made up his mind to strike across to the road which runs over the downs from Low Harbour to Castleton, the county town of Southshire.

About an hour's hard walking brought him to the Headquarters of the County Police at Castleton; where the inspector in charge, on seeing his card, received him with the same deference that the general medical practitioner pays to a Harley Street baronet.

An expedition was quickly fitted out, and before the afternoon was spent, the body of an unknown man was recovered from the stream and lodged in the Castleton mortuary.

At the inquest which followed, it was proved that the deceased was a man of medium height and good physique, between twenty-eight and thirty-five years of age, fair haired, blue-eyed, and clean shaven. Death had occurred eight or nine days previously and decomposition was fairly advanced. There were no marks on the body suggesting violence, except two slight scratches on the upper lip, which, however, appeared to have been inflicted after death. They were apparently made with a sharp instrument, such as a razor.

At this point the Coroner interposed with a question.

'Can you offer an opinion as to how long after the death these cuts were made?'

'At least two days,' replied Doctor Smythe, who had conducted the post-mortem.

'They had no connection, then, with the cause of death?'

'No.'

'What was the cause of death?'

'Mitral disease of the heart.'

'Can you suggest for how long the body had been in the water?'

'Probably at least four or five days.'

'Have you formed any opinion as to the meaning of the cuts on his face?'

'I am inclined to believe that the lip must have been shaved after death by a somewhat unskilled operator.' (Sensation in court.)

Evidence was given by the police to the effect that the deceased was clothed in a suit and boots of good quality, though they seemed to be too large for him: there were no marks on any of the clothes by which the names of either the owner or the makers could be identified, except in the case of the collar, on which, though part of the lining had been cut out, evidently to remove a name, it had been possible to decipher the maker's imprint which had become almost invisible owing to the effect of repeated laundrying. The name was Jones and Son, High Street, Hillborough.

The laundry marks had all been removed from the clothing; and the only contents of the pockets were stones, which had apparently been placed there to keep the body from rising to the surface of the water in the course of decomposition.

The verdict of the coroner's jury was 'death from natural causes'; but a rider was added, urging the desirability of the police using every effort to establish the identity of the deceased, and to discover and bring to book the person or persons who had deposited the body in the stream where it had been found.

Inspector Candlish, whose holiday had been so rudely interrupted, was compelled to spend at Castleton, in connection with the inquiries about the unknown, many of the precious hours that he had dedicated to his beloved birds and plants. He removed his baggage from Low Harbour to a Castleton Hotel, and made that town the centre of his walks whenever he could escape the assiduities of the local police, anxious for his advice and support in connection with the, for them, quite unprecedented mystery which they had to unravel. Indeed, it must be said that the Inspector himself had been deeply intrigued by the unusual features in the case; and, even after the inquest was over, he found it difficult to get back to that serenity of mind and freedom from the cares and worries of life that are so necessary to those who would successfully explore nature's secrets.

The face of the dead man, inscrutable and questioning, was constantly in his mind, and after vainly trying to forget it for a whole day, and to recall his holiday mood, he resolved, having communicated by telephone with his superiors at the Yard, to devote the few days still left of his vacation to an attempt to solve the mystery.

His first action was to re-visit the spot where he had found the corpse: there he made a careful search, walking backward and forward over the expanse of grassland, about a hundred and fifty yards wide, that divided the road from the bank of the stream. The weather had been dry, and no footprints had been discovered when the ground had been first examined, nor was the Inspector more successful in this respect now; but in one place on the side of the road he found the marks of motor tyres pointing towards the river, as though a car had been turned round so as to run off the road on to the grass. It was his business to know all about such matters, and in the present case he was able to identify the impressions as having been made by a car with a plain tyre on the left front wheel, and diamond patterned Clincher tyres on two of the others: the fourth wheel had left traces too indistinct to tell any story at all.

His next move was to visit Hillborough on his way back to town, to get what information he could from the makers of the dead man's collar.

As every one knows, Hillborough is in Surrey, about twenty-five miles from London: not many years ago it was a typical country town, with a market on Saturdays, when the farmers' 'ordinary' at the County Arms brought together for combined sociability and business all the substantial yeomen of the surrounding district; but the growth of the metropolis is transforming sleepy old-world Hillborough, and the slopes of the

surrounding hills are becoming co
red-brick houses of well-to-do city men,
keepers are being elbowed out by branches
concerns as Kearton's Tea Emporium, the Home
Stores, and Boomer and Co., Limited.

The journey from Castleton to Hillborough takes a t
two hours, for fifty miles of cross country travelling, in the
Mid-Victorian trains which are considered good enough for
the south of England, counts for more than four times the
distance in one of the fine expresses that ply between London
and the north of England.

To pass the time *en route,* and at the same time to clarify
his own thoughts, the Inspector wrote down the following
questions in his note-book:

   (i) Who was the deceased?
   (ii) Who placed his body in the river?
   (iii) What was their motive?
   (iv) Why was the body dressed in another man's clothes
      and boots?
   (v) What happened to his own?
   (vi) Why was the moustache removed after death?

MEMS.

(*a*) To interview police at Hillborough as to anyone
     missing from the neighbourhood.
(*b*) To question Jones and Son as to collar.

The Town Hall and other public buildings at Hillborough,
including the Police Station, are situated at the bottom of the
market place, which slopes upward to the old parish church
standing at the summit of the small hill from which the town
takes its name: at the back of the Town Hall is a public recreation ground, by the side of which, in a walled enclosure, is
the mortuary; beyond these the ground begins to rise again and

the large houses in the

...orough Police Station was ...person with a tremendous ...ity of his position. To him ...an merely a means to earn a ...a sort of priesthood—a dedica- ...He believed firmly that the last ...ed in the British criminal code, ...him to have a deeper significance and a m... .... than the law of gravitation, while those 'rights' o... ....perty which it was primarily framed to protect were as abso... e and eternal as the very universe itself.

He put on his uniform cap with the same reverential ceremony as a bishop assumes when he dons his mitre at some great Roman Catholic ceremonial; he made entries in the station register as though he were a sibyl writing in the book of fate; and when he gave evidence in court, it was as if Zeus himself had descended to earth to utter oracles.

This remarkable functionary was able to hide from the world his very slow-witted and infertile mind by his deliberate manner, his ponderous dignity, his dogmatism, and his sincere belief in himself; which qualities had earned for him promotion and a reputation for wisdom.

It was not the first time that the detective had had dealings with policemen of the Dyson type, and he knew that the administration of a little judicious flattery is the one way to manage them.

After introducing himself, therefore, he said: 'I am proud to make your acquaintance, Inspector, your reputation reached Scotland Yard long ago. I have come down, charged by my superior officers to seek your advice and co-operation in a difficult inquiry.'

'I shall be glad to tender you any assistance that lies in my power,' was the reply.

'Well, first of all I want to ask if anyone has been missing from this district: the body of a man has been found in Southshire, and there is some reason to think he may have come from these parts, as his collar bears the imprint of a Hillborough tradesman.'

Inspector Dyson reflected and replied, 'No, I can safely assure you that no one whatever has been reported missing in this part of the country for a considerable period.'

'Then,' said the Scotland Yard man, 'can you tell me anything about Jones and Son of High Street, Hillborough, whose name was on the collar?'

'They are the principal men's outfitters in the town,' was the reply, 'very respectable, old established tradesmen. If you would like me to do so, I will gladly introduce you to Mr Jones, Senior, who is a member of the Constitution Club, to which I consider it my duty as a public servant to belong.'

This offer having been readily accepted, the two Inspectors proceeded together to High Street, to the establishment of Jones and Son; and after the distinguished Londoner had been introduced and his mission explained, the two officers were invited to a cosy room behind the shop, where Mr Jones examined the dead man's collar and pronounced it to be size sixteen and a half, of a shape for which there was a large local demand: theirs was for the most part a cash trade, and of this they kept no detailed record: there were certainly dozens of men in the neighbourhood who wore collars of that shape and size.

With this purely negative result Candlish had perforce to be satisfied, though, with an eye to possible future exigencies, he allowed his country colleague to think that his assistance had been of the greatest value.

Finding he could just catch a train to town, he declined the latter's proffered hospitality, promising, however, to let him have news when the mystery was finally solved.

The next morning saw the Inspector back in his office at

Scotland Yard where, once more absorbed in the succession of routine duties, the vivid impression made on his mind by his holiday adventure began to fade.

Neither the notices that had appeared in the Press, nor the advertisements and inquiries of the police, brought in any information about the dead man, who might have dropped from the clouds, as he appeared to have belonged nowhere and to nobody on this earth.

CHAPTER III

'For thee I'd scale the highest Alp;
    I'd swim the ocean wide,
I'd storm the very gates of hell
    To win thee for my bride.'
                                    BALLAD

ABOUT a week after Inspector Candlish's visit to Hillborough
and subsequent return to town, Basil Dawson, who as a
pressman was obliged to reverse the old saw, 'early to bed and
early to rise,' was lingering over his ten-thirty breakfast in his
chambers at Pump Court, Temple, when his telephone bell
rang: taking off the receiver he recognised the voice of Doris
Lyttleton; and as she spoke he caught a note of strain and
anxiety in her tone.

'Is that you, Basil? Do you know I am dreadfully worried
about father? I showed you the cable I received from him
announcing his safe arrival in New York. Well, that's over a
week ago, quite time enough for a letter to have reached me;
but not another line either by post or telegraph has come. When
he has been away before, he has always been so good about
writing. I do hope that nothing can have happened to him.'

'Don't allow yourself to get nervous, dear,' was Basil's reply,
'I am quite sure your father's all right. He is an old hand at
travelling, and knows how to look after himself. I expect he is
having an extra busy time and has not had much opportunity
for writing. Suppose you come up to town to lunch with me.
I'll lay myself out to cheer you up; and it will do me no end of
good to see you. What is more, we will lay our heads together
and concoct a cable to your father to tell him how much you
want to have news of his doings.'

15

Doris readily assented to this proposal; and for once was induced to forgo the uncertainty and hustle of an X.Y.Z. café for a quiet corner table at Jacobini's in Soho.

Giuseppe Jacobini is a most attentive host, and something of a character. His early experience as a hotel chef has given him a first-hand knowledge of cooking, cookables, and cooks, of which his customers enjoy the benefit. A meal at his restaurant is given an additional savour by the cordial manner of the host, who makes a point of visiting every table and greeting each comer as though he or she were an old family friend.

There are two ways of lunching at Jacobini's: those who want the utmost possible value for two shillings, have the table d'hôte, a feast in five courses, more distinguished perhaps for quantity than for quality, but without doubt satisfying to even the most robust of appetites. The fastidious, however, feed 'a la carte,' where everything is of the best and the price higher accordingly.

Basil was aware of the fact (though neither he nor any other philosopher has ever succeeded in explaining its cause) that no Italian can make coffee, so he resisted the persuasive waiter who wished him to order a pot of the mysterious liquid which passed under that name at Jacobini's, and introduced Doris to the merits of a glass of Freisa as a substitute.

Under the cheering influence of a good lunch, and the pleasant conversation of her fiancé, Doris began to feel that she had been making a mountain out of a molehill, and that her father was of course all right—'what could have happened to him in one of the best hotels in New York?' she said, 'even if he had met with an accident I should certainly have heard, as he always carries cards with his address on them in his pocket-book.'

After talking the matter over from every point of view, the lovers decided, in order to make assurance doubly sure, to send two cables—one addressed to Mr Lyttleton at the Grand Washington Hotel, New York, asking him to wire news of himself; and the other, reply paid, to the manager of the hotel, asking him to state if Mr Lyttleton, of London, was still staying in the establishment, failing which to telegraph any information he may have left at the hotel as to his future movements.

The cables were duly despatched; and when they parted, Doris undertook to ring Basil up as soon as she received a reply to either of them.

Between ten and eleven that night, Basil was sitting in his room at the *Daily Gazette* office, doing his share in the preparation of the next day's issue of the paper, and in no way disturbed by the roar of the great presses underneath, when the telephone bell rang, and in a moment he was listening to the very agitated voice of Doris explaining that she had just received a cable from the management of the Grand Washington Hotel, to the effect that her father had departed from there on the morning of the 8th of July, having made a stay of one night only. He had left no word as to his movements.

Basil tried successfully not to let the uneasiness he felt appear in his tone, as he urged Doris still not to be anxious, pointing out that her father had probably been called away to some other town—Philadelphia or Chicago possibly—and that she would certainly hear from him in a day or so.

As a concession to her disquietude, however, he proposed that he should meet her in good time the next morning to accompany her to her father's office in the City, as in all probability his partners were in touch with him and would be able to furnish his address.

'Good-night, dearest,' said he in conclusion, 'be sure to sleep soundly and don't worry.'

'That's easier said than done,' was the reply, 'but I'll try to take your advice—*Au revoir*, Basil.'

The following morning Basil, by dint of getting up an hour earlier than his wont, and forgoing his usual leisurely breakfast in favour of a cup of coffee swallowed as he dressed, was able to meet Doris in Old Broad Street at the entrance to Winchester

House, just as the clocks of the city churches were striking the hour of ten.

The firm of Lyttleton, Menzies, and Lyttleton occupied a handsome suite of offices on the first floor. Established in the late eighteen sixties, 'Lyttletons,' as it was called familiarly in the city, could not be compared with such colossi as Rothschilds or Barings, but it had risen steadily from small things to great, and was already a power in the inner circles of finance: there were few important flotations, few 'deals' of the first magnitude in which its influence was not felt; and it was said among the initiated that it had had at any rate some share in bringing about at least six wars—each of which had added to the prestige and resources of the firm, and at the same time expanded the boundaries of the British Empire.

For some years, owing to ill-health, Mr Menzies had taken but little part in the business, the direction of which he had left to his partners, James Lyttleton and Horace Lyttleton, his cousin.

Despite the close relationship in blood and business, Doris had seen but little of Horace Lyttleton and his family, and what she had seen had not inspired her with desire for a closer acquaintance.

Accordingly, when she and Basil entered the sumptuous general office, she asked to see Mr Saunders, the manager, instead of inquiring for her relative. An obsequious office boy, recognising her as the chief 'governor's' daughter, hastened to fetch Mr Saunders, who invited her with her escort into her father's private room.

David Saunders was about forty years old, slim and of medium height; his black hair was beginning to turn gray over the temples, and to grow thin on the crown. Like most high officials, bank managers, and solicitors, his face appeared to be a sort of conventionalised mask, hiding the presence, or absence, of a personality, in the background. Discretion, accuracy, trust-worthiness, caution, were virtues that appeared to radiate from him, but Mr Saunders was anything but a mere machine. He was a man of considerable ability and great ambition. He aimed at becoming himself a financial magnate; and had already begun to operate on the Stock Exchange on a fairly large scale. He was a bachelor and shared a comfortable house at Purley, in Surrey, with his younger brother Frederick, who participated in his ambitions and admired intensely his abilities.

Twenty-five years' service with the firm, during which period he had worked his way up from office boy at five shillings a week to manager at nine hundred pounds a year, had taught David Saunders that between a partner and his relations and a mere employee, there is a gulf of caste almost as wide and deep as that which in India sunders Brahmin from Sudra.

Doris, however, though 'born in the purple,' was not altogether spoiled by her father's wealth, nor forgetful that the richest are of the same clay as the poorest, and that the same red blood runs in the veins alike of the millionaire and the clerk; she therefore greeted Mr Saunders as an old friend and introduced him to Basil.

'I'm so worried about father, Mr Saunders,' she said; 'have you heard from him at the office since his arrival in New York?'

'We have only had one cable, Miss Lyttleton, and that was sent off by your father the day after he arrived in New York. It simply announced his arrival and stated that he would wire again as to the date of his return.'

'I don't know whatever to do about him, Mr Saunders, he went away the next day from the hotel where he stayed after landing in New York, and left no word as to where he was going: that is now nearly a fortnight ago, so there has been plenty of time for a letter to reach us from him. I do hope there is nothing wrong.'

'Would you like to see Mr Menzies? I informed him of Mr Lyttleton's absence, and he has been coming up to the office during the last two weeks.'

'Thank you, we will see him before we go. Is Mr Horace Lyttleton here?'

'No, Miss Lyttleton, he is still away on his holiday in France. I notified him by letter of your father's absence and told him that Mr Menzies was in charge.'

At this point Basil, who had been looking about him with the eye of a journalist trained to notice whatever was pertinent to any subject in which he was interested, picked up a 'Red Time-Table' which was lying on the blotting paper on Mr Lyttleton's table; and asked:

'Was this time-table here when Mr Lyttleton was last in the office?'

'Yes, the new time-table is placed on his table regularly on the first of every month and the old one removed. You will notice that this is the July number.'

'Has anyone else used it since he went away?'

'That is most unlikely, Mr Dawson, as there is another copy in the general office to which members of the staff can always refer if they wish to.'

'Then it is curious,' said Basil, 'that just before leaving for Liverpool, Mr Lyttleton should have turned down a page of towns beginning with "Hi" and should actually have made a pencil mark against the 4.10 train from Victoria to Hillborough.'

'My cousin, Horace Lyttleton, lives at Hillborough,' said Doris, 'perhaps he marked the book.'

'I don't think that is possible,' said the manager, whose voice and eyes expressed his surprise at the turn the conversation was taking, 'Mr Horace left for France before the end of June, and we have not seen him at the office since: I understand that his son is away with him and that he has shut his house up till his return.'

'I wonder if your father knew anyone else at Hillborough,' said Basil to Doris.

'I have never heard of anyone,' said Doris, 'he and cousin Horace were not at all intimate outside the office, and I have never known him mention Hillborough before, much less go there.'

Mr Saunders at this point suggested that he should inform Mr Menzies that Miss Lyttleton and Mr Dawson would like to see him.

'Well, darling,' said Basil to Doris, as soon as they were alone, 'there is only one thing for me to do and that is to get leave from my editor to run over to New York to see if I can obtain news of your father there.'

'That is nice of you, Basil; it would be a tremendous relief to me to know that you were going to find him for me.'

The door opened, and Mr Menzies entered. He was a delicate, scholarly-looking man, whose appearance was more suggestive of an Oxford don than a city financier, and who grudged the time he was occasionally obliged to devote to the city as being lost to the more essential task of writing a treatise on *Greek Coinage Designs from* 600 *to* 200 B.C. which he regarded as the real business of his life.

He greeted Doris as an old friend. 'My dear Miss Doris,' he said, 'I am so sorry that you are having all this anxiety about your father: he has always been the most precise and business-like of men as regards correspondence, and I cannot understand his prolonged silence. I feel sure, however, that there is some good and quite simple reason for it; and that it will not be long before we hear from him.'

'I hope so indeed, Mr Menzies, but let me introduce you to my fiancé, Mr Basil Dawson.'

'I know your name quite well, Mr Dawson, and am delighted to have this opportunity of congratulating you both,' said Mr Menzies. 'Mr Lyttleton told me all about your engagement when last I saw him.'

'Thank you,' said Basil, 'I certainly am to be congratulated. Do you know, Mr Menzies, we were just planning, when you came in, that I should go over to New York to see if I can get any news of Mr Lyttleton; but there is just one point that requires clearing up while we are here. I found this time-table on Mr Lyttleton's desk: the date proves that it was only in his possession for the few hours he was here before leaving for Liverpool; and yet he has turned down a page and marked a train going, not to Liverpool, but to Hillborough. Can you suggest any explanation?'

'I know nothing of Hillborough,' was the reply, 'except the fact that Mr Horace Lyttleton lives there; and as he was out of England on the 1st of July, I cannot imagine any reason for Mr Lyttleton wishing to go there. Most probably the mark was made by one of the clerks.'

After some minutes' further conversation, during which no one could make any suggestions of value, Doris and Basil took their leave: Doris to motor home to Long Vistas, and Basil to make the necessary preparations for his journey.

CHAPTER IV

'Who is this masquerader?'
The Belle's Adventure

As a journalist, Basil was accustomed to travel; and he was thoroughly well up in all the arts by which a journey can be made in the speediest and most comfortable way possible. His preparations therefore, did not take him long; and the evening saw him start for Liverpool to embark on the *Moldavia*, which was due to sail for New York early the next morning.

The voyage was pleasant and uneventful; and, but for his anxiety on Doris's account, Basil would have thoroughly enjoyed the five days of fresh air and sunshine.

He had arranged that Doris should send him a marconigram if news came to hand about her father; but no message came; and accordingly, as soon as the steamer reached her berth in the Hudson, he drove to the Grand Washington Hotel, booked a room, and sent in his card to the manager with a request for an interview on urgent business.

The interview was accorded; and the manager, Mr Julius M. Smith, 'some hustler,' as his subordinates called him, listened to his story, and when he had finished, rang through to the office and asked a clerk to bring in the register in use on July the 7th.

'I recollect quite well, Mr Dawson,' said he, 'receiving Miss Lyttleton's telegram last week, but I am very much afraid I can't add to the reply I sent then; however, you shall see the register for yourself.'

The book arrived; and after some search, Basil discovered the entry 'James Lyttleton, London, England.'

'But this is not Mr Lyttleton's handwriting,' said he. 'May I ask your clerk one or two questions?'

'Why, certainly,' said the manager, as he gave the necessary instructions through a speaking tube.

'Johnson,' said Mr Smith, when the clerk entered the room, 'I want you to answer any questions Mr Dawson here may put to you.'

'I understand,' said Basil, pointing to Mr Lyttleton's name, 'that you were in charge of the register on the 7th of July when this entry was made.'

'I guess that's so,' was the reply.

'The handwriting is not Mr Lyttleton's: can you explain that?'

'Sure,' said the clerk, 'I wrote the name myself. I remember quite clearly what happened. Mr Lyttleton came up to the desk, and said he had just arrived from England and wanted a room. I requested him to register. He said he had cut his finger and asked me to do it for him, which I did.'

'Was there any other conversation between you?'

'He asked if there were any shows worth going to up town; and I told him that *Misses and Kisses* at the Madison Empire was just first rate. He thanked me and said he thought he would look in at it.'

'*Misses and Kisses*,' said Basil, 'that sounds like a very light musical comedy; I should not have thought it would appeal to a staid old gentleman like Mr Lyttleton.'

'He did not look too old or too solemn when I saw him,' said the clerk.

'He's over sixty,' said Basil.

'I should have guessed thirty-five.'

'But his hair is quite gray.'

'My impression is of a man well under forty,' said the clerk; 'if I had seen gray hair I should have put him down for much older. The only sign of age I noticed was his bad eyesight. He seemed to find a difficulty in seeing things, although he wore spectacles.'

'Did you see him when he left the hotel?'

'No, sir, I did not,' said Mr Johnson, who then went back to his duties.

Basil felt a curious and undefinable excitement—much the same kind of feeling that he had had before in connection with some of his journalistic 'scoops'—a sort of presentiment that something would happen; that discoveries were impending if only he could continue to probe in the right direction.

'Now, Mr Smith,' he said, 'if you are willing, I would like to see the chambermaid who attended to Mr Lyttleton.'

The manager assented and rang through the necessary instructions to the chief housekeeper. A few minutes later a trim, collected, observant-looking young woman entered the room.

'The housekeeper told me you wished to speak to me, sir,' said she, addressing the manager.

'Were you in charge of number six hundred and eighteen on the second floor on the 7th of the month?'

'Surely, sir, I was.'

'Then will you please answer any questions this gentleman may wish to ask you,' said Mr Smith, indicating Basil, who opened fire at once.

'Do you recollect an oldish gentleman arriving at the hotel on the 7th who stayed in number six hundred and eighteen for one night only?'

'Well, sir, there are so many coming and going in my rooms, that it is not easy to bear them all in mind.'

'He came straight off the steamer from England, does that help to recall him?'

'I can remember a gentleman arriving from England about that date, sir, I noticed the label on his trunk, but he did not strike me as being oldish.'

'Can you describe his appearance?'

'He was fairly tall, and I think was clean shaven and had dark hair. I could tell he was not an American by his accent, but there was nothing very striking about his appearance, except that he seemed very near sighted.'

'What was his trunk like?'

'It was a large leather one, almost quite new.'

'Were there any labels on it?'

'I only noticed the steamer label, sir.'

'Did you notice his clothes?'

'He was dressed as a gentleman, in a dark suit, but I didn't pay very much attention to him.'

'Did he leave anything behind him when he went away?'

The girl thought for a moment, then said hesitatingly: 'I think I remember that it was in his room I found a collar dropped down behind the dressing table, but I am not absolutely sure, sir. In any case, it was just about that time I found the collar and took it down to the clerk in charge of visitors' lost property.'

Here the manager, who had been listening intently, rang through to the office, saying, 'Send Miss Jacobs in to me at once with the lost property register.'

After a brief interval, Miss Jacobs, a bright, dark-eyed young woman, whose remote ancestors were natives of Palestine, appeared carrying a large book.

'Miss Jacobs,' said the manager, 'will you please turn up your entries for the 8th of July, and tell me if a collar was brought to you on that day by one of the chambermaids.'

'Yes, Mr Smith, here are the particulars: the collar was found in number six hundred and eighteen on the second floor, after the departure of a gentleman called Lyttleton.'

'Has it been claimed?'

'No.'

'Please bring it here.'

Miss Jacobs disappeared, and in about two minutes returned, carrying a collar in her hand.

The manager took it and passed it over to Basil, who examined it with great care and noted the following particulars in his pocket-book: 'A double collar, nearly new, size sixteen and a half, maker's name: Heath and Dickson, 230 New Bond Street, London—brand: The Improved Mayfair Collar.'

Miss Jacobs and the chambermaid having been dismissed, Basil took his leave of Mr Smith, after thanking him for his courtesy and helpfulness, and strolled into the lounge, where he rang for some coffee, lit his pipe, and settled down to think over what he had just learned and to plan out the next steps to be taken in his search.

He was beginning to feel that something was very wrong indeed: both the clerk and the chambermaid had described 'Mr Lyttleton' as being on the right side of middle age, though their evidence on the point was not absolutely definite and conclusive; yet Doris's father, though still active and energetic, with his gray hair, lined face, and somewhat pompous, author-itative manner, could hardly be taken for much less than his age, sixty-two, even by a very unobservant person.

Then again, both clerk and maid had remarked on the stranger's near sightedness. Mr Lyttleton, it is true, wore glasses; but other-wise his vision was very good. He certainly did not look like a man who had difficulty in distinguishing the objects about him.

The theatre incident, too, was quite uncharacteristic. Basil could not imagine his dignified father-in-law elect setting out gleefully to see a performance as frivolous as *Misses and Kisses* by its very title must be.

The suggestion was unavoidable that a much younger man was masquerading, for some unknown purpose, as Mr Lyttleton. What other evidence was there? The testimony of handwriting could not be appealed to because the visitor had pleaded a cut finger and the clerk had made the necessary register entry for him. This point again was not conclusive; but if the man was not the person he claimed to be, he certainly would, as a most obvious precaution, have avoided leaving his autograph script in the first place that would be examined by anyone making inquiries about the missing financier.

There remained the trunk and the collar as the only tangible and real bits of evidence, though the former might have been bought by Mr Lyttleton when, and if he decided to visit America in so hurried a manner. Anyway, both trunk and collar appeared to open up possible lines of investigation.

But, thought Basil, if the stranger was not Mr Lyttleton, who was he? and why was he masquerading here? where was he now? and, more important still, where was Mr Lyttleton? did he really go to Liverpool? If the cable he was supposed to have sent from New York was fraudulent, so might have been the Liverpool telegram. In that case it looked very much indeed as though there had been foul play, perhaps even murder.

Having reached this point in his excogitations, Basil rang the bell and asked for a cable form, on which, regardless of expense, he wrote the following message:

'Lyttleton, Long Vistas, Hampstead, England—Very hopeful of success. It will help me to know where your father bought his collars and what size. Did he take any trunk away with him?—BASIL.'

He then had a taxi fetched, drove to the telegraph office and despatched his cable; after which he told his driver to proceed to Police Headquarters.

The police force of the City of New York has been glorified, caricatured, or merely described in innumerable novels; while its members have appeared as heroes, villains, or pantaloons in hundreds of those very sentimental or melodramatic film dramas which come to us from the other side of the Atlantic; no attempt will therefore be made in this veritable narrative to describe either its offices, methods, or personalities. Suffice it to say that Basil, who pleaded the urgency of his business, was received courteously by a burly, wide-awake looking official, Police Captain Farrell, who listened carefully to his story, taking ample notes.

'I agree with you, Mr Dawson,' he said, 'that there does appear to be something very wrong; but, though we will do our best to help you, I do not think you will discover very much on this side: it looks as though Mr Lyttleton must have disappeared in England, and that the cable from the Grand Washington Hotel was intended merely to put you off the real trail until the scent had grown cold. I can promise you, however, to have inquiries made at once to see if the man who impersonated Mr Lyttleton can be traced after he left the Grand Washington. I will 'phone to the hotel as soon as we find out anything of importance. And for your part you might show me any reply you may get to your cable about the collar and trunk.'

Basil made his way back to the hotel, feeling tired in body and anxious in mind; baffled by the problem he had so light-heartedly set out to solve, and worried by the thought of the pain and trouble that lay before Doris.

Action is always an anodyne; but Basil could only wait, and waiting for someone else to act is trying even in everyday matters of no special importance; but when issues of life and death are at stake, a merely passive part is apt to become intolerably irksome. Moreover, he was a poet with a poet's imagination, and could realise only too vividly the sorrows and troubles of other people, especially of those he loved. He had, however, too much strength of character and vitality to give way to the blues for long; so he sat down and wrote a long, cheerful letter to Doris, giving her a humorous account of all the day's adventures, and by not so much as a hint alluding to his doubts and fears with regard to her father's fate.

The following morning Basil had again to undergo the ordeal of waiting inactive. A dozen times he sent a page to inquire if a cable had arrived for him; until at last, just after lunch, the long hoped for missive was handed to him. Tearing open the envelope he read:

'Dawson, Grand Washington Hotel, New York—Father bought all collars from Samuelson, Cornhill, size seventeen. He took no trunk from home nor office. Anxious for further news.—DORIS.'

'This turns my suspicion of foul play almost into certainty,' thought he. 'The man who occupied room number six hundred and eighteen on the night of the 7th of July, and left his collar behind him when he went away the next morning, was under forty, wore a sixteen and a half collar, and obviously had eye trouble, therefore he could not possibly have been Mr Lyttleton, who is over sixty, wears a seventeen collar, and has good eyesight for a man of his age. The pseudo Lyttleton is an Englishman who must have been thoroughly acquainted with Mr Lyttleton's home and office circumstances; it is almost certain that it was he who sent the telegram from Liverpool on the 1st of July; he must have crossed by the *Ruritania* and sent a cable to Doris on his arrival here; and by this time he is no doubt back safely in England, hoping that his ingenious little scheme will have put us right off the scent. The best thing I can do is to see the police again and then get back to England by the next boat.'

With this reflection, Basil went to the telephone and called up the Police Headquarters, asking to speak to Captain Farrell, the officer he had interviewed the day before.

'Is that Captain Farrell? Good day, Captain, my name is Dawson, you will remember our conversation yesterday about a missing English gentleman. Well, I have just received a cable that I want to show you. Can I see you if I come round to Headquarters at once?'

'Certainly, Mr Dawson, come right along. I have some news about the man who personated your friend that will interest you.'

'Coming now,' said Basil, replacing the receiver.

Quarter of an hour later he was shaking hands with Captain

Farrell, who asked him to sit down, and condescended to accept one of his cigars.

Basil produced the telegram.

Well,' said the official, 'this confirms the conclusion that we arrived at yesterday; I think, sir, that you will find your friend somewhere near London; and I would suggest that you lose no time in getting back and putting the case into the hands of Scotland Yard. In the meantime you will be interested to learn that we have found the taxi man who drove the impostor away from the Grand Washington. I had a notice circulated to the city garages and ventured to anticipate your wishes by offering $100 for information. Just a few minutes before you 'phoned, a taxi driver turned up to claim the reward. I have him waiting now in case you would like to see him.'

'I am greatly obliged to you, Captain, for your prompt action. You did perfectly right in offering to pay for news. I would certainly like to see the man.'

Captain Farrell pressed a buzzer and told the police officer who came to the door to bring driver Dahlman in.

Dahlman proved to be a stout, weather-beaten person of about fifty-five, whose complexion was the colour of old port, but he had the quick, alert eye and concentrated look of a man whose business it is to drive a swift automobile through the crowded streets of a great city.

The Captain motioned him to a seat.

'I understand that your name is Henry Dahlman,' said he, 'taxi driver of 429E South Eighty-Sixth Street, Yonkers, and that you are claiming the $100 offered in this notice.'

'You've got it correct, Captain; I guess that little reward is mine.'

'Well, go ahead with your story.'

'It was just about the middle of the morning, say between half-past ten and half-past eleven on the 8th of July—I remember the day because it was the birthday of one of the kids—I was crawling along slowly past the Grand Washington, looking for a fare, when the porter waved me up to the hotel. The fare turned out to be a gentleman in spectacles who blinked at me and told me to drive him to the Central Depot. I put him down for an Englishman from his stiff manner and finicking way of speaking. Well, I drove him up to the yard of the depot and he got out with his trunk and passed me up two dollar bills.'

'Is that all you can tell us?'

'Well, there is just this bit more—that same night when I was brushing out the cab, I found, tucked away under the seat, this pair of spectacles which I have been intending to hand over to the police. Of course, I can't be sure who left them there, but it may have been the man you are after. I didn't happen to notice whether he was wearing glasses or not when he paid me.'

'The spectacles ought to have been brought in the day after you found them,' said Captain Farrell sternly. 'We shall make one or two inquiries, and if your story is confirmed you will get the $100.'

At this point Basil intervened: 'Did you notice, driver, what your fare did after he paid you.'

'Walked off into the Depot carrying his trunk,' was the reply.

When Dahlman had departed, the Captain said:

'If our man was wearing spectacles that he had bought in a hurry as a superficial disguise, two things would follow: first of all his eyes would have looked sore and strained while he had them on; and, secondly, he would have disposed of them as soon as they had served his purpose. Both these conclusions seem to fit in with the facts; and probably he turned his face away while paying his fare at the Depot, so that the driver should not notice that he was no longer wearing glasses.'

Basil assented: 'Of course, Captain, you could not allow me to take the spectacles away with me,' said he, 'but would you let me have them examined by an optician, who could write me out a copy of the prescription on which they were made up?'

'With pleasure, and what is more, I'll take you to the very

man who will do the job in a few minutes. His store is just a stone's throw from this building,' replied the officer.

Taking up their hats, Basil and the police captain descended into the street, and two minutes' walking brought them to the premises of Vandenker and Co., opticians.

Captain Farrell sent his card in to Mr Vandenker, who speedily appeared to greet his visitors.

'Good-morning, Mr Vandenker, this gentleman is Mr Dawson of London, who wishes to ask your advice on a matter in which he is interested.'

'Good-morning, Captain. Glad to meet you, Mr Dawson. In what way can I help?'

'I want you to reconstruct for me the oculist's prescription from which these spectacles were made,' said Basil, holding out the glasses which had been left in Dahlman's taxi.

The optician held the spectacles up to the light, moved them round in circles, and compared them with lenses which he drew out of a plush-lined case; he then made some careful measurements of their width, and the breadth of the bridge; and finally he scrutinised the gold used in the frame by the aid of a powerful magnifying glass.

Having completed his examination, he drew out of a drawer a sheet of paper of the kind used for oculist's prescriptions, with a sort of chart of a pair of spectacles; on this he entered the measurements, the degree of astigmatism of each eye, and the strength of the lenses.

'This is what you want, sir,' he said, 'and in addition I may tell you that the spectacles were made in England, for the gold frame has the British official eighteen carat hall mark.'

Basil thanked Mr Vandenker, and took leave of him after paying his fee.

'The fact that the glasses were of English make is another link in our chain of evidence,' said he to his companion when they stood once more on the pavement.

'That is so,' was the reply, 'and now, Mr Dawson, if I may

advise you, you had better return to England by the next boat, and leave us to do what we can to trace the movements of the bogus Lyttleton after he arrived at the Depôt.'

'I entirely agree with you,' said Basil, as they re-entered Headquarters; and, after making the necessary arrangements for paying the taxi driver's reward, and for the communication of any information the police might be able to dig out, he took his departure, drove to the steamship offices and booked a berth on the *Mauretania*, which was due to leave for Liverpool the following morning

CHAPTER V

'A wealthy citizen of Tarentum offered to sell his soul if the devil would in exchange make him the richest man in the whole of Italy; but Satan replied, "Sir, if you possessed a soul you would never have become rich; I regret, therefore, that as you have nothing to barter, I cannot trade with you."'

BALDACCHI'S *Tales*

BASIL had heard of the American family who 'did' all the picture galleries in London, including the Academy, with St Paul's Cathedral and Westminster Abbey thrown in, between late breakfast and early lunch; but he wondered if anyone had ever 'done' the United States in quicker time than he had.

'Less than forty-eight hours,' thought he; 'must be just about a record.'

The Statue of Liberty was now beginning to fade into the haze of the horizon: it was early afternoon; the weather was fine; and the lunch had been a good one. Basil felt his spirits begin to rise as he sauntered idly about the deck of the great steamer, puffing meditatively at a cigarette and allowing the stream of his thoughts to meander at will.

The rush and worry of the last two days seemed to be left behind with the fast receding land; no doubt he would find troubles, difficulties, and anxieties waiting for him at the other side of the ocean; but that other side was still a long way off; and the land, with its crowded cities, its hateful contrast of wealth and poverty, its insincere politics and social injustice, its gourmets and its starvelings, appeared infinitely remote and unreal, as he gazed out upon the gently moving waters

35

of the Atlantic, so open, so free, so magnanimous, as he put it to himself.

But this mood could not last long. He had only to turn his eyes away from the sea to the crowded decks of the *Mauretania* to be brought back with a jerk to the unpleasant realities of life.

'A gay scene, is it not?' said a voice at his elbow.

Basil turned towards the speaker, and was aware of a tall, spare man, evidently about the middle thirties, whose accent was that of a man of culture, while his clothes proclaimed him American. His bright eyes twinkled with intelligence and cynical good humour behind a pair of pince-nez; and between his strong, clean-cut jaws was fixed a large cigar which appeared to be contributing to his enjoyment of the scene.

'Yes,' replied Basil, 'I am inclined to fancy that Solomon in all his glory would look rather faded among these ladies.'

'Solomon,' said the stranger, 'why, sir, he'd be altogether a back number; there are at least fifty men on board this steamer who could buy him up, temple and all, and not know they'd spent anything.'

'I suppose they are a rich crowd.'

'Yes, sir, they are that: made so much money out of war contracts, or pre-war swindles, that they can't spend enough in the States to feel that things are moving at all, so they're off to Europe to splash their dollars about. Do you see that bilious looking old dyspeptic over there with the fat woman in pink—that's old Hiram van Splitz who owns about five hundred million dollars. How do you think he got them?'

'The political economists would say by the practice of thrift and abstinence,' said Basil.

'Theft and impudence would be nearer the mark,' was the reply. 'He came to New York at the age of nineteen, with empty pockets and with no education in particular: he has never invented anything, never made anything, never done a day's useful work, never said nor thought anything worth while, but by sucking other men's brains and exploiting their labour, has acquired wealth almost beyond compute, and through it such mastery over the bodies, minds, and destinies of thousands of men as an Asiatic despot might envy; and now he's off to England to buy a duke for his daughter who started life as Sally but now calls herself Sara, spelled without the final aitch.'

'You seem to be interested in the subject,' said Basil.

'I am that—in fact I am on this ship now on my way to England, in order to study the habits of the American and British upper classes at close quarters.'

'You find them worth studying?'

'Yes, sir, they tickle my sense of humour and I hope to get valuable sociological data for a book I am writing.'

At this point the stranger brought out his pocket case and handed Basil a card on which was printed the name Burton James, which Basil recognised as that of a rising and brilliant young novelist and playwright, whose work was beginning to be known on both sides of the Atlantic.

'I am honoured to make your acquaintance, Mr James,' said Basil, who produced his card in turn. 'I myself am also of the order of scribes, though I hope neither a Pharisee nor a hypocrite.'

The two men shook hands cordially, and paced up and down the deck together.

'After all,' said Basil, 'old Van Splitz should not be looked down upon in aristocratic circles: if he is not the descendant, he is at least the ancestor of gentlemen.'

'Unless gentlemen become obsolete in the meantime.'

'That may be in Russia under the Bolsheviks,' said Basil, 'but I cannot believe it will ever come about in England, where gentility is the national ideal, and with few exceptions every one either claims to be or aims to be a gentleman or lady.'

'Have you ever known a man or woman give any definition of the terms "gentleman" and "lady" that did not include themselves?'

'No, I suppose I never have: in fact, I have never succeeded in getting an intelligible definition out of anyone.'

'You may wager on it you never will,' said the American, 'whatever meaning the expressions may have had in the past, they have long since degenerated into cant words by the use of which every snob in England or the States is able to fancy him or herself better than other people.'

'If gentility is a mere shadow, there is no doubt that the substance of aristocracy in all countries alike is a big bank balance,' said Basil. 'Wealth carries with it education, health, and leisure, from which flow refinement and cultivated taste. The plutocrat's son becomes an aristocrat: the aristocrat stripped of his money sinks into the plebeian crowd. Gold is itself a philosopher's stone that transmutes red blood into blue.'

'But is it not somewhat anomalous that all the good things you have enumerated should go to men who contribute practically nothing to the common welfare, while the people who create all wealth must be thankful if they get enough of it to ensure a bare existence?'

'Yes,' replied Basil, 'but are we not getting dangerously near to Socialism, the profession of which I understand is considered a criminal offence by your countrymen?'

'There are a great many of my countrymen, Mr Dawson, who would be delighted to have me in prison for the remainder of my life; the comments on them and their ways in some of my books have so touched them on the raw. I take it as a testimonial to the usefulness of my work.'

As the voyage proceeded, the acquaintance between Basil and Burton James began to ripen into friendship: they spent a large part of their time each day walking up and down the long expanse of the *Mauretania*'s deck, drinking in health and vitality from the sparkling air which seemed to be flecked with gold by the sun's rays though kept fresh, cool, and sweet by the gentle sea breezes.

As they walked they discussed many things, and Basil told the American about the disappearance of his future father-in-law, which had been the occasion of his hurried visit to New York.

'A man who wished to disappear from his friends might frame up such a scheme himself, but I take it your fiancée's father was not that kind?'

'The very opposite,' was the reply. 'He was rich: his business was prosperous: he was socially inclined and had a large circle of friends: he was not the kind of man to entertain a doubt as to himself, his mode of life or any of his opinions. No, he was the last man to disappear of his own free will.'

'Had he any enemies?'

'I have never heard mention of such.'

'A rich man can scarcely fail to have made enemies. I should begin my quest, if I were you, at his offices and in his business circles generally.'

'I am afraid I shall have to turn the search over to the police,' said Basil, 'as my editor will expect me to get back into harness on my return. It was awfully good of him to let me have time to go to New York and back.'

'In any case, it would be worth while to look in at one or two of the most likely hotels in Liverpool to see if you can pick up any clues. Either the real or the false Mr Lyttleton must have stayed there for a night.'

The voyage came to an end at length, and Basil parted with his newly made friend, whom he urged to visit him at Pump Court within the next day or so. He then looked up the trains, found one which allowed him an hour or so in Liverpool, and sent off a wire to Doris accordingly.

As Mr Lyttleton's first telegram had been despatched from Lime Street Station, it was at that hotel that Basil made his first visit of inquiry; and sure enough he found that, much as had happened at the Grand Washington, a man had arrived and had asked the clerk to fill up the register for him in view of an alleged cut hand: on the separate form which at that period the Defence of the Realm Act required to be filled up by hotel visitors, Mr Lyttleton's home and office addresses were correctly entered. None of the hotel staff had apparently taken any particular notice of the guest, who had done nothing and left nothing behind him which could throw any light on his identity.

It was late that night when Basil arrived at Euston Station, but ten o'clock the following morning saw him at Long Vistas, where he received from Doris as warm a welcome as even an eager lover could desire.

'But, darling boy,' said she, when the first ecstatic greetings were over, 'what about father? I have been so anxious. Where is he? What has happened? Tell me quickly.'

'You are the bravest girl in the world, and I am just going to tell you the whole story,' said Basil. 'It is very disquieting, but I have not lost hope, nor must you.'

Basil then recounted the story of his quest, relating all his discoveries in New York and Liverpool; but touching lightly on the alarming deductions he had been compelled to draw from them.

'Now, dearest,' he said, when he had finished, 'we have got to set in motion every possible machinery for finding your father, and the very first thing I am going to do is to see my old friend Candlish, who is high up at Scotland Yard: if anyone can find him, he can.'

'But, Basil, what do you think can have happened to father? Do you think he has been kidnapped and held for ransom?'

Basil feared worse things than this; but he was glad that

Doris should not anticipate the worst while it was still uncertain, so he replied that her conjecture seemed to be the most likely solution of the problem. Then, promising to return after he had been to Scotland Yard, he took his leave.

CHAPTER VI

'It is by the patient accumulation of apparently trifling facts
that the most important generalisations are achieved.'

DEVILLE'S *Prolegomena*

IT was now nearly a month since Chief Inspector Candlish had
returned to the routine of the Criminal Investigation Department
after the very unsatisfactory ending of his holiday in Southshire;
and under the pressure of more immediate tasks, the first vivid
impressions of the mysterious tragedy in which he had accidentally become involved were beginning to fade from his mind.
From time to time, however, he would turn from the work of
the moment and open his pocket-book at the page where he
had written out the list of questions during his journey in the
train from Castleton to Hillborough. With a frown on his forehead, the great detective would read them through to himself
and wonder if he would ever be in a position to answer them.
On the whole, he thought it was unlikely; the journalistic stir
at the time of the inquest had brought no one forward to identify the body; no young man whose description tallied with that
of the corpse had been reported missing; and every day that
elapsed made the mystery deeper, the puzzle more insoluble.

While thoughts such as these were drifting through his mind,
a knock sounded on his office door, and he was asked if he
would see Mr Basil Dawson, of the *Daily Gazette*.

'Certainly,' said the Chief Inspector, 'show him straight up.'

Basil and Candlish were old acquaintances: they had been
brought into contact on several occasions when the Press and
public were unusually interested in one of the detective's more
spectacular cases; and they now exchanged the courtesies
suitable to the occasion.

'It's no go, I'm afraid, Mr Dawson, I've nothing on of the slightest interest to the public; all our brightest criminals seem to have chosen July of this year for their holiday. You newspaper men are insatiable. I don't know what you would do if murder and the other deadly sins went right out of fashion.'

'In that case we should have to write articles on the deplorable condition of out of work detectives,' said Basil with a laugh. 'But seriously, Inspector, I have come to ask your help professionally in a very urgent matter.'

The Inspector pulled his chair up to the table, opened a large note-book, selected a pen, and said: 'Tell me all about it, Mr Dawson, and, if I can help you, I will.'

Basil then went right through the history of James Lyttleton's disappearance, beginning at the conversation with his daughter before he left home on the 1st of July, and ending with his own discoveries in New York and Liverpool.

His narrative was interrupted from time to time by the questions of his listener, who appeared anxious to know every detail, even those that to Basil seemed most trivial and unimportant.

'There is just one question I would like to ask Miss Lyttleton before going further into the case,' said Inspector Candlish; 'do you think I could get through to her on the 'phone?'

Basil gave the necessary information, and a connection was made with Long Vistas.

'Is that Miss Lyttleton?—this is Basil. I shall be with you very shortly and you shall have all the news then. In the meantime, Chief Inspector Candlish is anxious to ask you a question. I will get him to come to the line.'

The detective then took the instrument and said, 'I want to ask what your father did with the letters he read at the breakfast table on the day he went away.'

After a momentary pause the reply came.

'He put them into his pocket and took them away with him.'

'Thank you. I hope I shall have reassuring news for you soon.'

After Basil's departure the Chief Inspector saw his superior officer, and went through with him the principal points of the story he had just heard, suggesting that, as he had no other pressing work in hand, he should himself make inquiries in the Lyttleton case.

The necessary consent was readily given; and the detective adjourned to his favourite café to fortify himself by a substantial lunch before beginning work on his new case.

As it was at his office at Winchester House that Mr Lyttleton had last been seen, Candlish made up his mind to make his first inquiries there. Accordingly, when he had finished his meal, and had set a light to a pipeful of his favourite smoking mixture, he boarded an inner circle train at Westminster Bridge and eventually arrived at Liverpool Street Station, which, as every one knows, is the nearest to Winchester House.

Although it was the last day of July, and theoretically the very height of summer, London, true to ancient tradition, was wearing her usual garments of gray: 'It's all the same beastly dismal colour from the sky down to the pavement,' thought Candlish, as he emerged from the 'Underground.'

A few minutes later he was standing at the inquiry counter in Lyttleton and Company's offices, where he sent his card in to Mr Horace Lyttleton, who had, he was informed, returned from France some days previously.

Mr Horace was prepared to see him, and he was ushered into a large room, furnished handsomely in the heavy style that is always affected by those who are, or would like to be, leaders in the world of banking and finance. The thick Turkey carpet, the mahogany furniture, the great safe in the corner, the walls covered with dark, embossed paper—everything suggested solid, old-established wealth—even the pictures seemed to tell the same story.

In the middle of the room, like an island in the sea, or an oasis in the desert, was a large knee-hole mahogany writing table; and seated at it facing the door was Mr Horace Lyttleton.

As this gentleman was inviting him to be seated, the Inspector was, according to his invariable custom, taking his mental photograph.

He saw before him a stout, though still active man of about sixty, clothed in a well-cut black morning coat, with perfectly creased pin-striped cashmere trousers. A neat pearl pin appeared in the exact centre of his black silk tie, a monocle hung from his neck; and in his button-hole was a pale mauve orchid. But the detective was particularly struck with the financier's face—this was large, with somewhat prominent gray eyes, and small side whiskers, and was rounded off by fat, clean-shaven cheeks; a large bald spot crowned his head; and but for the heavy jaws and somewhat predatory nose, all the features suggested joviality and benevolence.

'Well, Inspector,' said he in a hearty tone and with a smile, 'what has brought you to the city today?'

'I am making inquiries as to the disappearance of your partner and relative, Mr James Lyttleton; and I shall be most obliged by any assistance which you, sir, can give me.'

'Disappearance of Mr James Lyttleton! Why, I understood he was in New York on some private business. What do you mean by disappearance?'

'There is reason to suppose that he never went to New York at all, that he never left the neighbourhood of London in fact.'

'Nonsense, man, we had a cable from him after he arrived in New York. I have been expecting for days now to hear that he has returned to town.'

'Perhaps,' said the Inspector, 'I had better begin at the beginning and tell you the circumstances which have led Miss Lyttleton, your partner's daughter, to call in the assistance of Scotland Yard.'

The detective thereupon gave a brief account of the cable sent by Doris to the Grand Washington Hotel management; of the reply that was the cause of Basil's visit to New York; of the general trend of his discoveries there; and of the conclusions quite legitimately to be drawn therefrom.

'Well, this is a most extraordinary story,' was the comment, 'surely there must be some mistake somewhere! Besides, who could have played such a trick as to impersonate my partner?'

'That is just what I am anxious to find out. May I ask you a few questions, Mr Lyttleton?'

'With the greatest pleasure; but I can't help thinking that when my cousin turns up he will be annoyed that the police have been invited in to investigate his movements.'

'What is Mr James Lyttleton's position in this firm?'

'Senior partner: he is owner of a half share; Mr Menzies of a third, and myself of a sixth. Menzies, however, has always been more or less of a sleeping partner; and the control of things has been in the hands of my cousin and myself.'

'Had your cousin any enemies?'

'None that I know of. Of course, business in the city means competition; and an unsuccessful competitor naturally feels a little bitterness sometimes at his rival's good luck; but my cousin was a straight man who, though he hit hard, hit always above the belt; and that sort does not make enemies.'

'Had he any specially worrying business on hand recently?'

'I know of none connected with the firm; whether he may or may not have had private anxieties, I am not in a position to say.'

'You and he were not intimate friends then, if I may ask the question?'

'We were excellent friends in the office,' was the ready reply, 'but our tastes were dissimilar, and we saw very little of one another outside.'

'Had your cousin any connection, business or otherwise, with anyone resident at Hillborough?'

The financier's mouth opened in surprise, and his prominent eyes stared as he replied, after a moment's pause:

'Hillborough, why should you suppose he had business there?'

'Because the last thing he did before leaving this office was to look up and mark a train from Victoria to Hillborough.'

'I can't believe it,' was the reply, after a slight hesitation, 'why, my own house is at Hillborough; but it was shut up from the middle of June until my return from France a week ago. No, I certainly cannot suggest any reason why my cousin should have visited Hillborough. In fact, I don't believe for one moment that he did so. How do you know he marked the time-table in the way you suggest—I may have marked it myself.'

Mr Horace Lyttleton's manner was such as to suggest that he resented the introduction into the investigation of the name of the town he himself lived in.

'A strong local patriot, no doubt,' thought the detective, as he replied:

'The time-table was for July, and I understand that you went out of town at the middle of June, so it could not have been your doing. Now I need not trouble you further at the moment, but I should be grateful if you would allow me to question one or two members of your staff—your manager, in particular.'

'With pleasure, I'll have him in here now,' said the financier, ringing a bell.

Mr Saunders entered the room, and was asked a number of questions with regard to how Mr Lyttleton was dressed on the morning of his disappearance, and as to the possibility of the timetable having been used by some member of the staff. The Inspector took elaborate notes of his replies, and eventually took his leave.

At three minutes past six o'clock that afternoon, on his way down Old Broad Street to the Tube Railway Station at the Bank, Mr Saunders happened to meet Chief Inspector Candlish for a second time: the meeting appeared to Mr Saunders to be quite fortuitous; but the detective, had he been questioned on the point, would have quoted one of his favourite maxims, 'even chance can be planned.'

'Good-evening, Inspector,' said the manager, 'have you been able to find out anything about Mr Lyttleton yet?'

'Not very much so far, Mr Saunders, but that reminds me that there are one or two little matters which you can clear up for me better than anyone else. If you could spare a few minutes, we might have a little chat over a cup of coffee.'

Mr Saunders appeared nothing loath; and the two men turned into an X.Y.Z. café, where, in a corner of the smoking room they settled down to consume an infusion of the Arabian berry, and to smoke two of the Inspector's cigars.

'I suppose you miss Mr Lyttleton at the office, Mr Saunders,' said the latter.

'Well, it is the quietest time in the year just now,' was the reply, 'but undoubtedly we shall miss him badly later on, if he does not come back.'

'He was the chief partner, was he not?'

'Yes, and between you and me, the brains of the establishment. Mr Menzies is not interested in business matters, and Mr Horace, for all his imposing appearance, is not nearly up to his cousin in ability.'

'Had Mr Lyttleton any enemies, do you know?'

'I never heard of any. Mr Horace is not exactly universally popular in the city, where there are rumours that his private speculations have been unfortunate, and that he has lost a lot of money of late; but I never heard anyone speak against Mr James.'

'You consider then that he was anything but a quarrelsome man.'

'Never heard of his quarrelling with anyone—well, perhaps—I am not sure that I ought to mention it, but he and Mr Horace had pretty sharp differences of opinion occasionally.'

'But they were pretty good friends on the whole, were they not?'

'No, I am afraid I can't say that—but, look here, Inspector, you'll keep it to yourself that I have ever discussed my principals with you.'

'You need have no fear on that account,' said the detective.

'Anything you may be able to tell me about Mr Lyttleton, may be of value in my search for him. You were speaking about his relations with his partners.'

'Mr Menzies and he were always on excellent terms, and I believe visited each other outside the business, but there was a good bit of friction between the two Mr Lyttletons.'

'Was that or any other matter connected with business weighing on Mr Lyttleton's mind?'

'No, he generally appeared to be cheerful enough.'

'What did he usually do with the letters he brought up from home with him in the morning?'

'Those that concerned the business he would dictate replies to in the ordinary way: private ones he would answer himself, and either lock up in his desk or safe, or destroy, according as they might be important or not.'

'Do you remember whether he brought any letters with him on that last morning?'

'I didn't see any; but he came earlier than usual and was in his room when I arrived.'

'Do you know why he came so early on that particular day?'

'I have no idea.'

'Was any member of the staff there when he arrived?'

'A commissionaire and one of the office boys always come on duty at nine o'clock to attend to early telephone calls and sort out the post before the office opens at nine-thirty.'

'Can you recall anything Mr Lyttleton said or did that day?'

'Yes, he got me to send one of the clerks to the bank to cash a cheque for a thousand pounds on his private account.'

'Which bank was it?'

'The Broad Street branch of the Amalgamated Bank of Great Britain.'

'Was there anything unusual in his manner?'

'Now you mention it, he did appear to be a bit worried: he cut me rather short when I went in to get his instructions on one or two important letters which had just come in.'

'Did he dictate any letters outside the ordinary routine of business?'

'Not that I know of.'

'What time did he go out?'

'He went out to lunch about his usual time, one o'clock, and left about an hour or so after his return, say, somewhere about three or half-past.'

'And now, Mr Saunders, I think that is all; but I am going to ask you to find out from the commissionaire and office boy, who were in the office early on the 1st, what time Mr Lyttleton arrived, and what he did on arrival. I am asking this because I wish to avoid giving rise to talk in the office, which would be the case if I were to come in myself and ask questions.'

'I will do as you ask tomorrow morning, with pleasure, and I will drop you a line as to the result,' was the manager's reply.

By this time the dregs of the coffee were getting cold in the bottom of the cups, and emerging from the café, Mr Saunders and the detective parted on the most cordial terms, to go on their respective ways.

'It is a very curious thing,' said Chief Inspector Candlish to himself, 'that whatever work I am on of late, I constantly hear the word Hillborough. The dead man in Southshire bought his collar there; Mr Lyttleton looked up a train to Hillborough just before he disappeared; Mr Horace Lyttleton lives there; and yet there does not appear to be the slightest connection between the three events.'

Two mornings later, Candlish received the following letters:

'WINCHESTER HOUSE,
OLD BROAD STREET, LONDON, E.C.
August 2nd, 19—

'DEAR SIR,—As arranged at our recent meeting, I have questioned the office boy, Smith, who was on early duty on the 1st ultimo. His account is that he came in at 9 a.m.

as usual, and a few minutes later (he could not be more precise) heard the outer door of Mr Lyttleton's room slam; almost immediately afterwards the door between that room and the general office was opened, and Mr Lyttleton said that he was expecting a telephone message and that as soon as a ring came for him the caller was to be connected up to the extension in his room. Almost immediately the phone rang, and someone, who refused to give a name, demanded to speak to Mr Lyttleton. Smith made the necessary connection. He could not help hearing, he states, a word or so of the conversation that took place, for Mr Lyttleton's voice was raised and he seemed excited and angry. The boy heard the expressions "dissolution," "clear out altogether," "absolutely final." The commissionaire confirmed the statement as to Mr Lyttleton's early arrival, but he could give no other particulars.

'I trust that this information may be of value.
'I am, dear sir,
'Yours faithfully,
'DAVID SAUNDERS.'

AMALGAMATED BANK OF GREAT BRITAIN,
289A OLD BROAD STREET,
LONDON, E.C.
August 2nd, 19—

Confidential.

'DEAR SIR,—Referring to your call here yesterday, I beg to inform you that a cheque for one thousand pounds on the private account of Mr J. L. was cashed over the counter on the morning of the 1st ultimo, ten Bank of England notes for one hundred pounds each being tendered in exchange. The numbers of these notes were 987351-60

inclusive; and inquiries made this morning at the Bank of
England show that all of them have already been paid
through the London Agents of the Central National Bank
of New York, who state that they received them from their
head office in New York City.

'Yours faithfully,

'CHAS. JAMIESON,

'Manager.'

After reading these letters carefully and making some
entries in his pocket-book, Candlish wrote a letter to Police
Captain Farrell (the officer Basil had come into contact with
in New York) asking him to endeavour to trace the ten one
hundred-pound notes.

CHAPTER VII

'Unimportant details—nonsense, sir, there are none such. Give me enough details and I will explain the secret mechanism of the stars.'

JACKSON'S *Founders of the Royal Society*

HOLLY Lodge, Hillborough, the residence of Mr Horace Lyttleton and his son Myles, was a pretentious, modern red brick house, standing about forty yards back from the road, from which a semi-circular drive led up to the front door. At the back of the house was a large garden sloping downwards from the house to the boundary wall, which shut it off from the recreation ground at the back of the Town Hall and the adjoining enclosure wherein stood the chapel and other buildings of the borough mortuary. At the back of the house overlooking the garden, was a veranda into which the smoking and drawing-rooms opened. The view from this veranda was a delightful one. Across a well-kept lawn, bordered with deep beds of old-fashioned flowers—sweet william, hollyhocks, sunflowers, great clumps of lavender, bushes of sweetbrier, crimson ramblers, and others too numerous to specify, one looked between the old oaks and elms which shaded the lower part of the demesne, and saw as a background the picturesque public buildings of the little town.

The garden, which was enclosed by high brick walls, was not overlooked: one side of it abutted on a quiet road which led from the new part of the town to the bottom of the Market Place; and on the other side the spreading branches and thick foliage of a magnificent chestnut effectually screened off the windows of the adjacent house.

It was four o'clock (Willett time) on a Sunday afternoon at

the beginning of August, and the relentless rays of the sun made even the garden of Holly Lodge stifling and comfortless. Horace Lyttleton and his son were, however, doing their best to enjoy themselves despite the adverse circumstances. Dressed in delightfully cool-looking flannels, they lounged in deck chairs on the lawn in the shade of the great chestnut. Between them was a wicker table on which was a bottle of a famous whisky, two siphons and a large basin in which a pile of pieces of ice was rapidly disappearing.

By the aid of two choice cigars, they were fairly successful in warding off the attacks of the midges, gnats, flies, and other persistent insects that love the taste of perspiring human flesh on a hot day in summer.

There was a distinct family likeness between father and son, allowing for the difference of twenty-eight or so years in their ages. The younger man was lean and athletic in build: he had the paternal jaw and nose: his lips and neck were a little too thick: generally, he suggested a man prone to dissipation, but knowing exactly where to draw the line between enough and too much.

'There's only one way out of it, Myles,' said the older man, waving his cigar, 'you have got to marry that girl, or we shall both be in queer street. You and I, my boy, are used to living comfortably; and funds are getting disastrously low.'

'I am quite willing to marry her or any other woman tomorrow,' said the dutiful son. 'I don't want to pick and choose, as long as the lady is rich enough; but Doris has never seen me, and what's more is already engaged to another man, so I am afraid that if my marriage to her is the only remedy for our fortunes, we are in a bad way.'

'She has got to be made to marry you if she won't do it willingly,' said the older man. 'Providence removed her father just when things in the city were beginning to look really dangerous for me: the markets have been against me pretty steadily for some time past, and I have had to mortgage my interest in Lyttletons. If you marry Doris, however, my interest will become practically merged with her father's, for you will come in as partner in respect of your wife's share, and between us everything can be put right. The alternative is that I shall have to sell my share of the business; and when my debts are paid, there will be nothing left; and that would mean poverty for both of us and the end of all those little pleasures to which you are accustomed, my dear boy.'

'In that case, governor, we had better lose no time in calling on my sweet cousin: you can play the heavy uncle part, coming to offer condolences in her loss, while for me it will be a case of love at first sight! If that fails to score a bull's-eye, we must try some other tactics.'

At that moment there approached through the veranda a dignified looking manservant, holding in his hand a tray on which was a visiting card.

'Gentleman wishes to see you, sir, on very urgent business, so he says; wouldn't take no for an answer when I told him you never see people on Sundays.'

Mr Horace Lyttleton took up the card and read:

'Chief Inspector James Candlish, Criminal Investigation Department, New Scotland Yard.'

'An official of his standing should know better than to expect me to see him on a Sunday afternoon. I suppose I had better hear what he wants, though; show him round, Phillips, and bring another chair and glass.'

Candlish was duly introduced to Mr Lyttleton, Junior, and invited to sit down and partake of a whisky and soda and a cigar.

'Many thanks, sir,' said he, 'but if you don't mind, I'll light up my pipe. Thank you, just about a finger of whisky.

'I must apologise,' he continued, 'for disturbing you gentlemen at so inopportune a time; but, as you know, I am in charge of the inquiries with regard to the disappearance of Mr James Lyttleton, and some points have arisen on which you can perhaps help me.'

'I still think that New York is the most likely place to find him,' said Horace, 'but in any case I am only too anxious to help you. Poor James was a relative and friend as well as a partner in business; and I have been terribly worried about him since you told me what you suspected and feared.'

'Well, sir,' said the Inspector quickly and incisively, 'we have traced your cousin to Hillborough.'

'To Hillborough,' said father and son together breathlessly.

'Yes, gentlemen, to Hillborough. We have found the taxi man who drove him from Winchester House to Victoria Station, and one of the ticket collectors at this end remembers collecting a first-class ticket from a gentleman exactly answering to his description, who came down by the train leaving Victoria at 4.10 in the afternoon, and arriving at Hillborough at 4.50. Unfortunately, the 1st of July happened to be the local market day, and the town was very full, so I am afraid it will be difficult to trace his movements after leaving the station; unless you can make any suggestion on the point.'

'Why do you think my son or I could throw any light on the matter? The fact is, we were both in France at the time, and this house was shut up. I am afraid I cannot suggest any reason for my cousin's visiting Hillborough. I only wish I could.'

The Inspector was perforce obliged to accept this assurance, and after the butler had been summoned by the ringing of a bell, took his leave and proceeded to follow that functionary into the house through the veranda.

As he passed through the smoking room, his eye fell upon a brass newspaper rack in which were a number of old journals.

'Would you allow me to take one of these old newspapers?' said he to the butler. 'I am going on from here up to the woods on the other side of the hill, and I hope to find some ferns for my window boxes in town; an old paper will be just the thing to wrap them up in.'

'As many as you like, sir,' said the butler.

'Thank you,' replied the detective, picking up one of the papers which he proceeded to fold prior to placing it in his pocket. But suddenly he stopped, looked carefully at the paper, and turning to the butler, said: 'By the way, isn't it a bit dangerous to lock up a fine house like this for a month, when so many burglars are about?'

'My Lyttleton seemed to think it quite safe, sir, he got the local police to keep an eye on the house, and gave all of us servants a holiday.'

'I suppose no attempt was made to enter the house—you found nothing disturbed when you got back?'

'No, sir, everything was quite O.K.'

When Chief Inspector Candlish had got safely out of sight of Holly Lodge, he pulled out of his pocket the paper he had picked out of the rack in the smoking room, read the heading of the front page, then opened it out and examined the other pages in turn.

'The *Daily Telegraph* for the 1st of July, 19—! Well I'm blowed!' was his very unprofessional comment. 'And the house was empty and locked up for a fortnight before and a fortnight after that date.'

So much was the detective moved by this discovery, that he forgot all about his intention to spend a happy hour or two in the woods searching for ferns, but instead, strolled meditatively back through the Market Place to the County Hotel, where he had booked a room the previous afternoon.

There were scarcely any guests in the hotel. It was the day before the bank holiday, and the ubiquitous tribe of commercial travellers had all departed to spend the long weekend in their own homes. Except for two or three single men and a married couple or so who had come down to play golf on the famous Hillborough links, the capacious, old-fashioned hostelry was empty; and Candlish found that he had the smoking room all to himself when he rang for tea on his return from his call at Holly Lodge.

The bell was answered by a cheerful-looking, stoutish man of about fifty, who had discarded his coat, apparently because of the heat, and who wore an apron tied round his well developed waist.

'Just the man for local gossip,' thought the Inspector, as he ordered his tea.

After an interval of about ten minutes, the waiter returned with a tray well stocked with appropriate viands.

'Hot afternoon, sir,' said the waiter.

'It is indeed,' was the reply, 'it's lucky for you that you are not very busy just now.'

'I prefer it a bit more lively than this, sir; I am a London man myself, born and brought up in Hammersmith, sir, and I find Hillborough a dead and alive sort of place to be in always.'

'I should think it was, but still it is a pretty little town; and I expect you have a fairly comfortable berth here.'

'Not much to complain of as far as that goes, sir, but the place itself is so dull; nothing ever happens, except a church or chapel concert, or missionary meeting now and again. There is a cinema in the Market Place, it's true, but they get only old films that are so worn as not to be worth looking at. And then the people themselves—countrified is what I call them—they don't look at things as you and I might, but any bit of nonsense is enough to excite them—I suppose they've nothing better to think about—why, a lot of them actually believe in ghosts.'

'Well, ghosts are certainly a bit out of date,' said the Inspector, 'though I have heard that there is a society of professors and other big wigs in London formed for the purpose of looking for them.'

'They had better come down here then and see if they can catch Mrs Whiteley's ghost,' said the waiter with a chuckle. 'The people here have talked about nothing else for the last month. I'm fair sick of their silliness, sir; and now that it's come to the Town Council spending a whole evening jawing about it, well, I think it's about time someone came down from London to show them what a pack of fools they are.'

'It certainly sounds rather extraordinary,' said the Inspector.

'Extraordinary; not at all, sir, if I may say so: it all comes from a silly woman's fancies—how anyone with a grain of sense can listen to her rubbish, I can't think. You see, sir, it happened like this—but perhaps you wouldn't care to be bothered with it.'

The detective saw that the man was bursting to tell his story, and as he wished to lead him on to talk about other matters, he told him to go ahead.

'Well, sir, it's like this: we had a young gentleman from the colonies—New Zealand it was—staying here for a few weeks this summer. He told us that his grandfather had been a native of these parts, and he had come on a visit to the old country, as he called it, and wanted to see the place where all his people came from, as far as he could trace them out. Well, sir, he took a bit of a fancy to this district and stayed in the hotel from about the middle of May to towards the end of June: he used to go out walking to all the villages round about—fair mad he was after old churches and such like—every man has his own peculiar tastes, for my part I prefer a well-built modern house with the latest improvements—but that's as it may be—well, sir, this young gentleman, Mr Austin, it appears had a diseased heart; and one day he must have overdone himself tramping about, because he got back to the hotel quite exhausted; and as he was going upstairs to his room, he fell down dead. Well, sir, dying that suddenly, there would have had to be what they call a post "morting," but for the fact that Mr Austin had put himself under Dr Jennings of Church Road soon after he came to Hillborough; and the doctor was able to give a certificate. Of course, this being a hotel, the other guests would not have liked a corpse to be in the house, so the body was taken off to the mortuary down there by the Town Hall.

'Mr Austin had plenty of money with him to pay all expenses of the funeral; and Mrs Johnson, the landlady here, sent a telegram to his relations in New Zealand. Now she is a very kind lady is Mrs Johnson, and she could not bear to think of that poor young gentleman being buried all those miles away from his belongings without so much as a flower on his grave; so the day before the funeral, she sends a nice wreath round to Bill Whiteley, the mortuary keeper, to be placed on the coffin.

'Now this is where that silly ghost comes in. The coffin, ready nailed up, was lying on trestles in the little chapel at the mortuary; and Mrs Whiteley, wife of Bill Whiteley, is ready to swear that she took Mrs Johnson's wreath and placed it on the coffin at the head; but in the morning, so she says, when she unlocked the chapel doors, the wreath, instead of being where she left it, was moved to the foot of the coffin. Then she, being a bit hysterical, like most women, runs off to her husband, screaming out that a ghost must have moved the wreath in the night. Now Bill had had too much to do with corpses to take any notice of ghosts, so he tells the old woman that she must have been dreaming: at that she calls him an unfeeling brute, and rushes off to get sympathy from some of her female friends in the town; and before you could say "Jack Robinson" the story was all over the place. Some believes the yarn, others don't, and they gets jawing and arguing to such an extent that you may say all the natives are now divided into two parties, one siding with Mrs Whiteley, and the other with Bill. And at last week's meeting of the Council Alderman Jones, the chemist from High Street, gets up to propose that the vicar should be asked to what they call "exercise" the ghost; and the members debated on it, some sticking up for the ghost and others pooh-poohing it, till at last the Town Clerk, Mr Dickson, gets up and tells them that as there was no mention of ghosts in the standing orders, there was nothing they could legally do about it; and as it was by that time past nine o'clock and the Mayor wanted his supper, the Council had to adjourn and leave all their business over till after the holidays.

'That's the story, sir, and silly enough too, to the ears of London men such as you and I, if I may take such a liberty, sir.'

'It could hardly have happened in a large city, I admit; but haven't I heard that quite a number of Londoners live in the newer part of Hillborough, and go up and down to business every day?'

'That's quite true, sir, nearly all those big houses on the hill beyond the Town Hall belong to well-to-do city men— stockbrokers and the like.'

'Some of them must certainly be "warm" men, judging by the houses they live in. For example, what a fine place that is just at the rear of the Town Hall.'

'You mean Mr Lyttleton's house, sir, the one standing at the corner of Hill Road and Holly Road. A very fine place it is. They say that Mr Lyttleton is a big man in the City of London. But he doesn't keep up the style he used to. I am told that he has only a butler and a couple of maids, though he had eight or ten servants in the place when his wife was alive; but nowadays he and his son live up there in a very quiet way.'

'He has a son then?'

'Yes, sir, Mr Myles Lyttleton, the son, is a great golfer: he does not seem to do much but amuse himself. Bit of a ladies' man too, they say. Between you and me, sir, I may say that the two gentlemen, father and son, are not very well liked in the place; though of course, being rich, they are respected.'

By this time the detective had finished his tea; and the loquacious waiter reluctantly removed himself with the tray. It was not often that he found an intelligent listener who would, with a show of interest, allow him to talk for so long.

The remainder of the evening, with an interval for dinner,

Inspector Candlish spent with his notebook before him, absorbed in thought, which was interrupted only when his pipe required re-charging.

'The key to the mystery is here in Hillborough,' was his final verdict before retiring to bed, 'and if I don't find it within a mile radius of Holly Lodge, I'll eat my hat.'

CHAPTER VIII

'Man-traps and spring-guns!
Faith, this wood is full of snares.'
The Genoese Lovers

IT was the morning of bank holiday; and, although only ten o'clock, the torrid August sun was already blazing down fiercely upon the Market Place at Hillborough, which looked more somnolent than ever.

The shops were all shut, and their owners had not yet shown any overt signs of life beyond the opening of front doors just wide enough to admit cans of milk and morning newspapers.

Chief Inspector Candlish had made up his mind to celebrate the festive occasion by a judicious compromise between his profession and his hobby; so he had arranged to spend the morning and afternoon until tea time, trying to find someone who remembered seeing the missing Mr Lyttleton after he had left the railway station on that fatal 1st of July. And in the evening he would feel himself free to pursue his darling hobby—natural history—in the lanes and woods outside the town.

The Inspector was a firm believer in the maxim that 'good food means good work.' He had accordingly breakfasted generously and well; he had smoked a morning pipe over the *Daily Gazette*, and when he walked out of the hotel he felt, like the Antient Pistol, that 'the world was his oyster.'

In the Market Place the only persons to be seen were one or two leisurely traders putting up stalls for the sales of bananas, buns, and bottles of ginger beer and other such beverages, dear to the heart of the temperance reformer, but deleterious to the stomach of anyone over fourteen years old.

By the side of the drinking fountain in the middle of the Market Place, a small but enthusiastic band of Salvationists were tuning their instruments as a prelude to a big bank holiday soul-saving campaign. As the detective passed them, he paused a moment to watch and listen. The meeting was just beginning, and after a very bloodthirsty hymn (at least the word 'blood' seemed to be repeated in every line) had been sung to a music-hall tune to the accompaniment of two cornets, a trombone, three accordions, a big drum, and a pair of cymbals, an old gentleman with a long white beard began to preach, walking up and down and hurling his words like bombs at the Inspector and half a dozen children who were the only potential converts within hearing.

'Fifty years ago,' he shouted, 'I was a soldier of the King, wearing a scarlet coat; but now, I thank the Lord, I am a soldier of Jesus Christ, and I wear a scarlet jersey—'

Candlish did not wait for more, but began his monotonous task of inquiring from house to house along the route from the railway station to Holly Lodge, if anyone remembered seeing the missing man.

He had taken the precaution, as soon as he arrived in the town on the previous Saturday evening, of calling on Inspector Dyson at the local police station, not that he anticipated getting help of any value from that ponderous but dignified officer, but because he wished to disarm in advance the opposition that might arise from the offended pride of a narrow-minded and conceited man who feels himself neglected.

The morning passed in wholly unsuccessful toil, but after lunch the detective went back doggedly to his task; and finally, after exhausting the possibilities of Station Road and the Market Place (which by that time contained a fair sprinkling of loungers, both male and female, who appeared to have nothing to do, nothing to say, and nothing to think about), he turned into the Hill Road, which led up past the side of the Town Hall to Holly Road.

In vain were his inquiries at the houses on the right side of the road: on the left side are no houses, but only the boundary walls, first of the grounds in which the Town Hall stands, next of the mortuary, and finally of the garden of Holly Lodge.

The mortuary keeper, then, was the Inspector's last hope; so he crossed the road and rang the bell at the great doors which shut in that very necessary but gloomy edifice. The bell was answered by an elderly man whose face suggested a battle-ground between a naturally humorous temperament and the sombre dignity of his official position; a pipe and shirt sleeves were the most noticeable part of his attire.

'This must be the redoubtable Bill Whiteley himself,' thought the detective, as he opened up the subject of his quest.

Mr Whiteley had, it appeared, no recollection of seeing anyone corresponding to the description of the missing man; but as he and the Inspector stood exchanging views on the weather and other topics of general interest, a motor-car turned down into the road from the Market Place.

The car was driven by Horace Lyttleton, who was on his way back from the golf club, where he had enjoyed a few rounds of his favourite game.

As he passed them, he became aware of the detective and the mortuary keeper apparently absorbed in conversation of a confidential nature. For some reason or other the sight appeared to irritate him: he gave a start which caused the car to swerve; and then pulling himself together, drove on towards home.

He turned the car into the drive and drew up at the front door. Then descending quickly he opened the door and hurried through the house into the garden, where his son was reclining lazily in a deck chair, enjoying meditatively the dissimilar but harmonious aromas of Havannah tobacco and Highland whisky.

'What, back already, governor; I did not expect you for another hour.' Then seeing the expression on his father's face, 'Something seems to have upset you.'

'That damned inquisitive fool from Scotland Yard is in deep confab with Whiteley at the mortuary gate. The whole place will be reeking of scandal before he has finished; and people will be saying that we are responsible for James Lyttleton's disappearance.'

The young gentleman sprang to his feet.

'We must put our thinking caps on, father,' said he. 'Let us go into the house where we can talk matters over quietly.'

Father and son crossed the lawn and passed through the veranda into the smoking room; and after carefully shutting both doors, sat down and were quickly absorbed in earnest talk on some matter which, judging by their tones and tense looks, they regarded as very important and strictly private.

They were, however, not destined to be undisturbed for many minutes, for, knocking on the smoking room door, Phillips the butler announced that Mr Saunders from the office had arrived to see Mr Lyttleton on urgent business.

'Tell him I will be with him in a few minutes,' was the reply.

When his employer entered the room where he was waiting, Mr Saunders apologised for disturbing him on bank holiday.

'You will remember, sir,' said he, 'that we were expecting an important cable from Buenos Ayres about the Argentine Central Copper Mines. As the matter was so urgent, I went to the city this morning and found this had arrived: I thought you would like to see it without delay, so I came straight down.'

'That was good of you, Saunders; I don't think, however, that we can take any action in the matter until tomorrow. But you must have a glass of whisky before you go back.'

Mr Saunders accepted the proffered hospitality, and in due course took his leave.

When Candlish found that neither the mortuary keeper nor his wife could give him any information as to the missing man, he was constrained to admit momentary defeat, and on the principle of *reculer pour mieux sauter*, he decided to withdraw from the field of action for the remainder of the day, so that he might have leisure to form a more effective plan of campaign for the morrow.

He accordingly strolled back to the hotel and washed the August grime from his face and hands preparatory to enjoying a generous and restful tea.

The meal over, he armed himself with field-glasses, collecting boxes and other paraphernalia dear to the naturalist, and set forth to employ the remaining hours of daylight in the quest, no longer of human quarry, but of birds, butterflies, and plants.

He had found by experience that by dismissing his work entirely from his mind for a while, he was able to return to it with renewed energy, clearer perception, and deeper insight. In fact, as he sometimes told his cronies, it was only when consciousness was wholly taken off a subject, that the subconscious mind was given a chance of working on it. He had more than once left a problem unsolved in order to go to sleep, or to read a novel, or to follow some other train of thought; and later on, quite unsought, the problem had come back into the stream of consciousness with its solution, clear, definite, and complete. So on the present occasion he hoped that the subconscious part of him would bring order into the chaos of more or less connected facts, vague suspicions, and half-formed theories with which his mind was stored.

By crossing the Market Place in front of the County Hotel at Hillborough, then turning down one of the streets which run out of it downhill to the right, one reaches in about three hundred yards the railway line, a foot-bridge over which leads directly on to a field path, running through rich meadows to the foot of a range of low wooded hills about two miles away.

With the burden of his work cast aside, and the fruitless toils of the earlier part of the day forgotten, the detective set out refreshed and cheerful. Had he paused to look back as he was crossing the railway bridge, he might have noticed that a very ordinary looking man, whose straw hat was pulled down over his eyes, was strolling along about fifty yards behind him. But Inspector Candlish was too keen on the delights of the charming country in front of him to have time for looking back; and, if he had, he might not have noticed one individual among the scores of townsmen and women bent on enjoying a country walk in the cool of the evening.

As the detective strode along the path through the meadows, the other man lingered on the bridge, lighting a cigarette and looking down lazily on the railway. Every minute or so, however, he glanced across the fields, and when he saw that the man he was following had got a long enough start, he set off after him at a brisk pace.

Inspector Candlish, in the course of his professional career, had on numerous occasions 'shadowed' other men; this was probably the first time that another man had 'shadowed' him, but he was so absorbed in the delightful sights and sounds of the countryside, that he remained wholly oblivious of the interest he had excited in the mind of the individual who was so patiently 'trailing' him.

Presently the ground began to rise, and a final stile brought the Inspector out of the open pasture land into a wood. Here he continued to follow the path, stopping every few minutes to observe the movements of a bird or to examine some plant that lay half hidden by the all-pervading brambles.

In this way he meandered along round the lower slopes of the hill until after about a mile he came to an opening in the trees, in the middle of which was a fairly large pond, and on it two water hens gliding placidly to and fro. The evening was by this time well advanced and the rays of the setting sun fell obliquely on the surface of the water, turning the tiny ripples made by the swimming birds into the appearance of molten gold.

The Inspector sat down to feast his eyes on the scene at leisure: he pulled out his pipe and began to charge it with tobacco. The influence of the evening and his surroundings was upon him: he felt like a man in a dream, and the poet hidden deep in the heart of every one of us—even policemen— began to assert himself.

Was it through some vague clairvoyance or because he heard a breaking twig or muffled footstep, that he turned round suddenly? Who can say? For even as he turned, a heavy stick descended on his head; and he sank to the ground stunned and helpless.

His assailant had taken advantage of the detective's slow progress through the woods, to creep up gradually nearer and nearer, and had finally sneaked right up to him to deliver his cowardly blow. He now stooped over the prostrate man and examined the contents of his pockets, replacing everything except a note-book and a sheaf of papers which were attached to it by means of a rubber band: these he transferred to his own pocket. Then the unknown drew a small revolver out of a hip pocket, aimed it at the Inspector's head, and turning slightly away as though he could not bear to look at the result of his murderous work, pulled the trigger. Turning again, he was aware of a stream of blood flowing down over the face of his victim.

'He'll never talk again, that's certain,' was his comment as he raised the body and pushed it over the bank into the pond. Then, without waiting, he threw the revolver into the water and hurried away into the heart of the woodland.

About a quarter to ten o'clock that evening, Inspector Dyson was seated in a comfortable armchair, enjoying a well-earned rest in the bosom of his family preparatory to retiring to bed. The great man had relaxed something of the awful dignity which was his during office hours: his ponderous uniform boots had given place to carpet slippers, a pipe was in his mouth, a large glass of stout, with a jug from which he replenished it from time to time, was within reach of his hand, while the current numbers of the *Daily Mail* and *John Bull*, which were the chief sources of his opinions, lay on the table in front of him.

His wife, a stout middle-aged woman, who looked flabby in body and malleable in mind, was sitting near him listening with awed pride to the remarks he occasionally condescended to make; and, during the intervals of silence, stitching busily away at needed repairs to the family linen.

The inspector had just been reading aloud extracts from an article by a famous Cabinet Minister, who was also a sensational journalist of the first water, on an alleged conspiracy of Sinn Fein, the Bolsheviks, and the Kaiser, to blow up St Paul's Cathedral, rob the Bank of England, and generally to harass and annoy the governing class of Great Britain: his most sacred feelings were outraged by this revelation of the baseness of mankind, his face went purple, his eyes bulged and his voice became scarcely articulate; at the word 'Socialist' he choked.

'I'd send every one of these blackguards to prison for life,' he said, 'and as for the Sinn Feiners, I would pass a law to do away with them altogether—what I can't—'

At this moment came a sharp knock at the front door.

'Who ever can that be at this time o' night?' said Mrs Dyson, as she put down her work and rose from her chair.

'An official high up, like myself, in the service of His Majesty's Government, is always liable to interruptions and distractions,' was the dignified reply of her spouse, as he deftly whisked the jug and glass into the sideboard out of sight of prying, irreverent or unofficial eyes.

The front door opened, Mrs Dyson was confronted by a sturdy looking young man in a tweed suit and gaiters, holding a bicycle.

'Is Inspector Dyson at home?' he said.

'Might I ask what your business is?'

'My name is Thorogood, from Thorogood's farm over yonder, off the Downville Road, and I wish to speak to Inspector Dyson on a private matter which is very urgent indeed.'

'Then you had better step inside ... My dear, here's someone to see you on very urgent business.' Thus saying, the worthy lady ushered the stranger into the domestic holy of holies, and retired herself to the solitude of the kitchen, where, like a good housewife, she was able to find solace for her thwarted curiosity in the performance of necessary tasks.

In the meantime the visitor introduced his business, saying, 'I come from a gentleman named Candlish, who has had a bad accident. He is at my father's farm and wishes to see you at the earliest possible moment on important official business. He said I was to be sure to tell you that not a word of this must be mentioned to a human soul—not even to Mrs Dyson.'

The inspector was so astonished at this announcement that he could only stare. He began mechanically to search his pockets for the note-book and well-sucked pencil so dear to members of his profession, when the stranger added:

'Perhaps you would like to borrow my bicycle, inspector. It is quite easy to find the way, and it is a light night; please do start quickly though, as poor Mr Candlish is very bad. I am going on now to get hold of Doctor Jennings, in order to take him back with me. Here's the machine. I'll stand it up against the door. See you later.'

Before the inspector could gasp out that he would call first thing in the morning, the young man had disappeared; it was too late to back out of his adventure, so he decided to see it through.

By nature and by training he was slow—slow in thought and slow in action. To him, as to the average solicitor, folly and haste, delay and wisdom were synonymous. Reason after reason, all equally cogent, arose in his mind in favour of waiting or of postponing his departure; but at last the reflection that the longer he put off starting, the later he would be getting back, conquered his irresolution, so he opened the kitchen door and said in a stern, mysterious tone:

'Important official business requires my attention, Mary, I must go out at once; you had better not sit up, as I may be late.'

After putting on his boots, he kissed the partner of his joys and sorrows, telling her to be sure to leave the stout on the table for his return. Then mounting the stranger's bicycle, he rode off into the night.

The way was familiar to him, and he got over the ground fairly quickly, arriving at the farm just as Doctor Jennings and young Thorogood drove up in the former's car.

The party were admitted to the house by Mr Thorogood, Senior, who said, as his son introduced the new-comers:

'I am glad you've come, gentlemen, the missis is sitting with poor Mr Candlish now, and we've both been very anxious about him.'

'I think, perhaps, I'd better go up at once,' said the doctor, who, suiting the action to the word, picked up his bag and asked the farmer to take him up to the sick man.

In about twenty minutes Doctor Jennings reappeared, and said, 'I'm afraid, Inspector, you won't be able to see this poor fellow tonight. He is drifting into unconsciousness, and I am very much afraid he's in for an attack of brain fever. He kept on repeating, "Tell Dyson to report to Scotland Yard— keep secret at Hillborough."'

'What's the matter with him, doctor?'

'He's had two wounds on the head. One of them looks to me as if a bullet had made it; luckily it glanced off the bone instead of going through it: another inch and he would have been done for. But how did he get to your house, Mr Thorogood?'

'Well, doctor, it was about nine o'clock, or a few minutes earlier, my missus heard a feeble rap at the door, and there she found this poor gentleman, dripping wet through as if he'd been in a muddy pond, bleeding at the forehead with blood all over his face, looking ghastly, you can imagine, and scarcely able to hold himself upright. Many women would have been upset, but my missus is a plucky one, so she took hold of him and drew him into the house, got him on to the couch, and then ran off to fetch me and my son, who were just looking round the farm to see that all the beasts were safe for the night.

'Between us we carried him upstairs and got his clothes off. He managed to get out that his name was Candlish, and that he wanted Inspector Dyson fetched at once, and he kept repeating that no one else must know of his being here. "Let them think I'm dead," he said over and over again.

'My missus tied a bandage round his head to stop the flow of blood till the doctor could be got here. That's the whole story, gentlemen.'

'Then he said nothing about what happened to him?'

'Not a word, but judging from the state of his clothes, which are hanging up in the kitchen, it looks as if he had fallen into the pond along yonder in the woods about half a mile away. Whether he fell in or was pushed, I can't say.'

'I am afraid there is nothing more I can do for him tonight,' said the doctor. 'I've tied up his head and given him something to make him sleep. I'll be round again first thing in the morning.'

'Before you go, doctor, I think we ought all to have a word together,' said the inspector. 'Mr Thorogood, will you ask your wife if she will favour me with her presence for a moment.'

When the whole company had assembled, Inspector Dyson turned to the farmer's wife and said:

'Have I your permission, madam, to invite these gentlemen to be seated?'

Anticipating her consent, he drew a chair to the head of the table, seated himself on it as though it were the veritable woolsack, and motioned the others present to sit down.

'Mrs Thorogood and gentlemen,' he said portentously, 'we live in gravely critical times, and I feel it my duty to give you a partial insight into the inner meaning of the events of the evening. In the first place, I must ask you all to take a strict pledge of secrecy.'

Murmurs of assent came from all present.

'Next, I must make sure that you are all of strictly British nationality and descent.'

More murmurs of assent.

'You will doubtless be surprised,' continued the police official, clearing his throat, 'to learn that the gentleman who is lying upstairs at death's door is no less a person than Chief Inspector Candlish of the Criminal Investigation Department, Scotland Yard, who has recently been making an important investigation in this neighbourhood. Now I surmise that the Chief Inspector must have provoked the enmity and revenge of some of those who are all the time engaging in seditious plots and conspiracies against this great Empire. I hope that I shall not be divulging too deep a secret when I tell you that there is at the present time an abominable combination of Bolsheviks and Sinn Feiners with the Kaiser, pledged to bring our country to ruin. Gentlemen, I think my esteemed colleague must have come across some offshoot of this intrigue here in Hillborough, and the villains have punished his attempt to thwart their plans by trying to murder him.

'It will be my duty to visit London tomorrow morning to report what has occurred to the Chief Commissioner of Police; in the meantime you will say nothing, and, please Heaven, by our humble instrumentality the throne and constitution of our beloved native land will be saved from the dangers that threaten them.'

At the conclusion of this ponderous harangue, the

inspector again cleared his throat, and looked as though he expected someone to move a vote of thanks.

'Good gracious me, what are we coming to?' said Mrs Thorogood.

'Well, I'm blowed,' said her husband and son in chorus.

Doctor Jennings said nothing, but looked incredulous.

CHAPTER IX

'Let Mammon's votaries say what they will,
A bounder gilded is a bounder still.'
                                    Lyra Satirica

THE morning after the events just recorded, Doris Lyttleton was sitting in the library writing some letters. The anxiety and strain of the past few weeks was beginning to tell on her appearance. Her cheeks were hollower and whiter than they ought to have been, and her eyes were framed in big dark semicircles.

Had she been certain that her father was dead, and that she had lost him altogether, she would have mourned him sincerely, missed his kindly presence and suffered all the sting and sorrow of irrevocable parting; but the wound would, as it were, have been open and healthy. Time, the great healer, would have softened her distress, and every day that elapsed would have modified the bitterness of her grief. Her first feelings of despair and hopeless regret would have been gradually transmuted into gracious and kindly memories, tinged with sadness, it is true, but bearable and even pleasant. But while her father's fate was wrapped in obscurity day followed day bringing not assuagement but a fresh burden of doubt and anxiety, which caused the wound in her mind to fester and rankle with ever renewed virulence.

Basil had been getting very anxious about her, and was fearful of a nervous breakdown if something were not done to relieve the strain. He devoted all his spare time to the endeavour to distract her mind from brooding over her father's fate. The lovers met every morning at Long Vistas or somewhere in town, had lunch together, and either strolled in the Park or sat in a café (on wet days) until Basil was obliged to make his way to the *Daily Gazette* office.

On the present occasion Doris was expecting him to turn up about eleven-thirty with his American friend, Burton James, whom he wished to introduce to her.

When, therefore, a few minutes after eleven, she heard a loud double knock at the front door, she thought it must be Basil and his friend a little before their time. She was accordingly surprised and disappointed when a maid entered the room and announced 'Mr Horace Lyttleton and Mr Myles Lyttleton. I have shown them into the drawing-room, miss.'

Knowing something of her father's opinion of his cousin, Doris's first impulse was to refuse to see him; but reflecting that he might have something important to say, might even bring some news of her parent, she thought better of it, and entered the drawing-room.

Horace Lyttleton and his son sprang to their feet, the former looking, as usual, as though he aimed at appearing the incarnation of wealth, benevolence, and good taste, but had missed the mark by a little; the latter, as spic and span as a Bond Street tailor could make him.

'My dear child,' said Horace, advancing with both hands stretched out, 'my poor dear child, your cousin Myles and I have been thinking so much about you. We hesitated for some time lest we should intrude too suddenly on the sacred privacy of your sorrow, but our great anxiety about your dear father and our sympathy with you would not let us stay away any longer. So here we are.'

Doris was so intent on avoiding the fatherly kiss that her relative seemed bent on bestowing, that she scarcely heard what he said, but turned with some relief to face the greeting of his son, which promised to be less effusive.

'I am your cousin Myles Lyttleton, Doris,' said he, as he shook her hand. 'I have known about you ever since you were born, and have longed to make your acquaintance. I hope we shall be great friends.'

'It is very kind of you to call, but I am afraid I am scarcely fit to see anyone just now; when father returns, as I hope he will soon, he will, I am sure, be glad to welcome you here.'

This mild hint was quite lost on the visitors, who looked as though they had taken root in their chairs.

'My dear child,' said Horace, 'that is just why we have come, it was so dreadful to think of you left here all alone in your trouble, and we felt that it would be a great comfort to you to have the support of your nearest, and, I hope I may say, dearest, relations.'

At this point the door opened and the maid announced: 'Mr Dawson and Mr James.'

Horace and Myles glared at the new arrivals as though they were intruders. Doris rose to greet them, and Basil presented his friend.

'It is indeed nice of you to have come to see me, Mr James, I have heard so much about you from Basil.'

'I am greatly honoured, Miss Lyttleton, and I need not say how delighted I am to make your acquaintance.'

'Cousin Horace and cousin Myles,' said Doris, 'I want to introduce you to Mr Dawson, my fiancé, and to Mr Burton James.'

The four men exchanged greetings—stiffly on the part of the first-comers, cordially on the part of the late arrivals.

'Mr Dawson and his friend will, I am sure, appreciate the fact that this is a family gathering, and see the propriety of renewing their call at a later and more suitable occasion,' said Horace in his best heavy father manner.

'Mr Dawson and his friend will do nothing of the sort, I hope,' said Doris quickly; 'they have come here this morning to lunch at my invitation, Cousin Horace, and I should not dream of allowing them to go away at once. Besides, if this were a family gathering who would have a better right to be present than the man to whom I am engaged?'

'But we were going to talk about your poor dear father,' said Horace.

'Mr Dawson is entirely in my confidence,' was the reply, 'and I am sure Mr James will excuse us. Do I understand that you have anything to tell me about my father, Cousin Horace?'

'Only to say, my dear child, that as his partner and relative I wish to place my services and my son's at your disposal. I am sure it would be the greatest comfort to your father to know that you were in close touch with those who are competent by their business experience and close blood relationship, to give you sound advice and effective support.'

'Thank you, Cousin Horace, I am sure you are very kind, but I am quite capable of looking after my own affairs.'

'Blood is thicker than water,' said Horace sententiously.

Burton James had been for some minutes looking questioningly at Myles Lyttleton, and at last said:

'I cannot help thinking that I have had the pleasure of meeting you before; have you been in New York recently?'

Myles Lyttleton looked surprised, and half turned towards his father; then pulling himself together, replied:

'You are mistaken, sir, I have never been in New York in my life.' Rising and addressing Horace, he proceeded: 'Now, father, we had better be getting back to town; I know you have an important meeting in the city at two o'clock, and things don't seem to be propitious for the quiet family chat we were hoping to have with Doris. Good-bye, Doris, I shall look forward to seeing you again in the near future. Good-morning, gentlemen.'

Anxious, apparently, to bring an unprofitable conversation to a close, Myles was out of the room almost before he had finished speaking. His parent followed after a farewell speech to Doris that he at least intended to be affecting.

Nothing was said until the sound of the shutting front door reached the drawing-room.

'Thank God, they're gone,' said Basil. 'Excuse my strong language, Doris.'

'I feel like using a stronger expression still, so you may consider yourself forgiven, Basil; but I am afraid that Mr James will have formed a peculiar opinion of our English family life.'

'Not at all, Miss Lyttleton, I quite understand the position. Dawson has told me all about it. I only wish I could be of some use to you.'

'What made you think you had seen Myles Lyttleton before, James?' said Basil.

'Just a passing impression: I was probably mistaken, and if Mr Myles has not been in the States, I certainly was wrong, for I have never visited Europe till now.'

'I wonder if Myles has been in New York,' said Basil. 'Could it have been he that personated your father, Doris?'

'What a mad notion, Basil! I don't profess to like Cousin Myles or his father, but we have no reason whatever for suspecting them of having anything to do with my father's disappearance.'

'I shall mention the matter to Inspector Candlish, all the same,' said Basil. 'I admit it is very unlikely, but every possibility should be explored—in any case, Myles was not in London for some time after your father's disappearance; he claims to have been in France, but he may have been in New York.'

'I don't agree with you at all, Basil: whatever motive could Myles Lyttleton have for kidnapping father?'

'I don't know enough about him to answer that question,' said Basil. 'But I am going to find out before many hours are passed.'

The conversation then drifted to more general subjects, and lunch was soon announced.

When the meal was over, Doris took her guests into a delightful little room, which she called her study, for coffee and cigarettes, in both of which she herself shared. Doris, being a woman, at once youthful and intellectual, regarded the cigarette, not from the merely material view as something to please the taste and soothe the nerves, but as a symbol of the emancipation of her sex, and therefore to be ranked with the Phrygian cap of the revolted galley slaves, which has become the badge of Liberty.

'With men cigarette smoking is a habit: with women a rite; men smoke because they like it, women because they think they ought to,' said Basil.

'There is something in that, Basil, but you forget that you men all began to smoke as boys; not because you thought tobacco tasted nice, but because you imagined that smoking was a "grown up" practice, and an assertion of manhood as against the assumption of your parents and schoolmasters that you were still children; but you took jolly good care to make your demonstration in private.'

'Quite right, Miss Lyttleton,' said Burton James, 'I remember when I was about twelve buying a pipe and some tobacco as a Christmas present for an uncle; and then, overcome by the splendour of the idea, taking it to a remote corner, and, trembling at my own temerity, smoking pipe after pipeful, till I felt thoroughly sick and miserable physically, but at the same time proud and happy at having so boldly asserted the dignity of my manhood before the universe.'

'I hope you were not found out: a flogging would have been a wretched ending to so glorious an adventure.'

'No, I was not found out. I took the precaution of eating some peppermint bullseyes on my way home, which effectually drowned the smell of tobacco, but even discovery and punishment would have left me something of the consolation that every martyr feels when he suffers for what he considers a good cause.'

'By the way,' said Basil, 'I have been wondering if that oculist's prescription I brought back from New York can be made of any use as a clue: it would be interesting, as a start, to compare it with your father's prescription; do you think you could find it, Doris?'

Doris said she would try, and in a few minutes came back with an envelope which she handed to Basil.

Basil took the prescription, opened it, and laid it down on the table beside the paper which he had obtained from Mr Vandenker.

Doris and Burton James stood beside him; and all three carefully scrutinised the two documents.

'They appear to be exactly the same in every respect,' said Burton James.

'I am afraid they are,' said Basil.

'Oh, Basil, what does that mean?'

'It means that the people who kidnapped your father took his spectacles and used them as a sort of disguise. I don't know that the discovery takes us much further though. We knew that some unknown man personated your father in New York; we have now proved, what we had already inferred, that he had actually been in contact with him before starting: in other words, that the man who went to New York had something to do with Mr Lyttleton's disappearance.'

'I think I shall go mad if this dreadful uncertainty about father continues much longer,' said Doris.

At that moment a maid announced that Mr Dawson was wanted on the 'phone. Basil went into the hall and put the receiver to his ear.

'Is that Mr Basil Dawson? This is Detective Sergeant Mitchell speaking from Scotland Yard. I want to see you urgently, sir, about the Lyttleton case.'

'I thought that Chief Inspector Candlish had the matter in hand.'

'I'll explain all about it when I see you, sir. Would it be

possible for you to call at the Yard this afternoon? Or, if more convenient, I could run up to Hampstead.'

'I'll taxi down at once and be with you within half an hour,' was Basil's reply.

He then returned and told Doris and Burton James what had taken place.

'I shall have to start at once,' he said, 'in order to get half an hour at the Yard on my way to the office. I am so sorry to have to hurry away.'

'May I come with you, Dawson?' said the American, 'perhaps I may be able to do something to help.'

'That is awfully good of you, old chap, I shall be delighted to have you with me. Will you excuse us, Doris?'

'I have already ordered the car for you,' said Doris, who had just re-entered the room; 'but whatever happens, don't forget to 'phone me. I shall be fearfully anxious till I hear what has taken place.'

The four or five miles between Hampstead and the Embankment were quickly covered by the powerful Rolls Royce car; and Basil and Burton James were soon ushered into Sergeant Mitchell's room at Scotland Yard.

'I am sorry to have had to trouble you, gentlemen,' said the sergeant, when Basil had introduced himself and his friend, 'but the fact is that Chief Inspector Candlish has met with a serious accident: a determined attempt was made yesterday to murder him: luckily it just failed; and there is every prospect of his complete recovery, but in the meantime he is down with a slight touch of brain fever, and the notebook which he always carried in his breast pocket is missing, so we don't know exactly how far he got in the case. We have his reports, the last of which was despatched on Saturday night, but the circumstances connected with the attack on him make it look as though he must have made important discoveries afterwards, and that the murderers or kidnappers of Mr Lyttleton must have been aware of it, and so made an attempt to suppress his evidence. We are making careful inquiries on the spot, but in such a way as to keep secret the fact of his escape, as we wish to leave the delinquents to imagine that they have been successful in silencing him; and I must ask you, gentlemen, to keep all that I have told you strictly to yourselves.'

The two listeners gave the required promise.

'Now, gentlemen,' continued the detective, a young, smart-looking man who was Candlish's favourite pupil and most brilliant assistant, 'I have gone carefully through the notes made by the Chief Inspector of his first interview with Mr Dawson, and his subsequent reports, of which I have made a short summary, which I propose reading through to you. Afterwards I shall be glad to hear any comments you may have to make, and I may ask you to supplement my information on certain points.

'PRÉCIS OF THE LYTTLETON CASE MADE BY
DETECTIVE SERGEANT MITCHELL.

'Mr James Lyttleton received a letter on the morning of the 1st of July, which caused him to leave home for his office half an hour earlier than usual. The contents of the letter were apparently of an unpleasant nature and probably included a statement that the writer proposed to communicate with Mr Lyttleton by telephone at his office at about 9.15 that morning. Mr Lyttleton reached the office and received the telephone message: he was evidently upset by what passed because he raised his voice and used expressions indicative of excitement and annoyance: he subsequently sent a clerk to his bank to cash a cheque on his private account for one thousand pounds. With this money presumably in his pocket, he left the office about an hour after his return from lunch.

'We have the evidence of the taxi-driver who picked

him up outside Winchester House about half-past three, and drove him to Victoria Station.

'He was subsequently noticed by a ticket collector at Hillborough as the only person arriving by the 4.50 train who gave up a first-class ticket. From that moment no authentic trace can be found of him; but, on the other hand, we have ample proof that an unknown man deliberately attempted to lay a trail of false evidence as to his purported movements. The telegrams from Euston and Liverpool on the 1st and 2nd of July, the cable from New York on the 7th, the entry in the register of the Grand Washington Hotel, were among the unknown's activities, and we may assume, as the notes Mr Lyttleton obtained from his bank before leaving the office were cashed in New York, that the man who personated him had first robbed him—'

'Excuse me,' said Basil at this point, 'I think I can add something to your information.'

He then proceeded to tell the detective about the spectacles which the pseudo James Lyttleton had left in Dahlman's cab, and how the prescription for them corresponded exactly with Mr Lyttleton's own prescription. The detective made a note of the point and continued reading.

'Since he paid the cabman and walked off into the Central Station, no trace of the impersonator has been discovered, though the New York police are making inquiries.

'Mr James Lyttleton was rich, his health was good, and he is not known to have had enemies: he appeared to enjoy life, and his mind and imagination were in a perfectly normal condition; it is therefore impossible to believe that his disappearance was voluntary or that he was himself a party to sending someone with his bank notes and wearing his spectacles to impersonate him in New York.

'We have then to answer the following questions:

'(1) Where is Mr Lyttleton?

'(2) What man or men are responsible for his disappearance?

'To deal with the second question first: the guilty person or persons must have been thoroughly acquainted with Mr Lyttleton's home and business circumstances; they must have had some motive for putting him out of the way; and they must in all probability have some connection with the town of Hillborough.

'Now Mr Horace Lyttleton is a partner and relative of James Lyttleton, and therefore has had unrivalled opportunities of knowing all about his home and office affairs; he was not, as we know, on good terms with his cousin; he is reported to have lost a lot of money in speculation; and this may have come to the ear of James Lyttleton and precipitated a row between the cousins— the phrases overheard by the office boy when Mr Lyttleton was speaking on the telephone on the morning of the 1st of July included the word "dissolution," which might easily be used by a partner who was angry with another partner; finally, Horace Lyttleton and his son live at Hillborough. There appears, therefore, to be a prima facie case against them.'

'I might add, gentlemen,' said the detective, putting down the sheets from which he had been reading, 'that Horace Lyttleton and his son were both supposed to be away in France during the period in which Mr Lyttleton disappeared, and long enough afterwards for his impersonator to get to America and back. Moreover, it was just outside Hillborough that the Chief Inspector was attacked yesterday evening. All these considerations together suggest very strongly that Horace and Myles Lyttleton are the guilty parties.'

'My friend here, Mr James, met Myles Lyttleton this morning, and was under the impression that he had seen him before in America,' said Basil.

'A very vague impression indeed, certainly nothing that your police could take as evidence,' replied his friend.

'Well, gentlemen, that is as it may be,' said Mitchell, 'but I was going to ask if Mr Dawson can give me any information about the Lyttleton family: especially about Horace and his son.'

'I am afraid I can't tell you very much about them,' was the reply. 'James and Horace were each sons of one of the original partners in the firm of Lyttletons. Horace inherited his share in the business some years after his cousin had been in virtual control as senior partner. Being a pompous, purse-proud sort of man, he was always jealous of James; and I gather they saw as little of each other as possible. I believe that on more than one occasion Horace tried to dictate a policy on some matter or other, and much resented being overruled by James, who invariably received the backing of the second partner, Mr Menzies. Horace inherited a large sum of money years ago when his father died, and used to live in great state at one time; but it is said that he is not nearly as well off nowadays.

'I think that's all I know about him, except that he and his son called at Hampstead this morning, tried to force themselves upon Miss Lyttleton as her father's nearest rela-tions and oldest friends, and talked a lot of insincere rot. I don't understand their motive, but from what I saw of them I wouldn't trust either of them out of my sight. They appeared to me to be just the sort to stick at nothing if they got into a corner.'

'Do you know where they were supposed to be staying in France?'

'I never heard, but you'll get the address from the manager at Winchester House—Saunders—who must have had it for forwarding letters.'

'Thank you, I will ask him for it. Well, gentlemen, I must thank you for your assistance. You will remember not to hint to anyone what I told you about my chief.'

Basil and his friend once more promised to be silent, and the interview closed.

CHAPTER X

'Beware of paper, pens, and ink;
Beware of talking when you drink;
Beware of saying what you think;
For many good fellows have swung in a noose
For letting their tongues or their pens run loose.'
The Highwayman's Legacy, 1751

SERGEANT MITCHELL held his superior officer in high esteem, and in taking up the Lyttleton case he felt not only his usual keenness to solve a mystery, but also a strong desire to avenge the violence done to his chief. He accordingly set to work with the utmost energy.

His first action on the following morning was to visit Hillborough, where he spent some days in instituting a search for the would-be assassin of his chief, and in other work connected with the Lyttleton case. Failing, however, to achieve any substantial result, he left the matter to the local police and returned to town. After reporting himself at the Yard, he went straight to the city and called at the offices of Lyttleton, Menzies, and Lyttleton, at Winchester House, where he asked to see Mr Saunders.

'Do you mean the manager?' asked the commissionaire at the inquiry counter.

'Yes, certainly; I do not know of any other Mr Saunders.'

'The manager is Mr David Saunders, and his brother, Mr F. Saunders, is also on the staff. I will ask Mr David Saunders if he can see you now.'

'I am an officer from Scotland Yard, can I have a few moments' private conversation with you?' said the detective, handing his card to Mr Saunders when that gentleman arrived at the counter.

'With pleasure; will you come into my room?' was the reply.

The detective accepted the proffered chair, and carefully laid his straw hat, gloves, and cane on the floor by his side.

'I am making inquiries in connection with the disappearance of Mr James Lyttleton,' said he.

'But you are not the gentleman who called here from Scotland Yard a few days ago.'

'No, that was Chief Inspector Candlish.'

'What has happened to him?'

'He has been unable to continue work on the case,' was the non-committal reply. 'I want to ask you, Mr Saunders, if you can let me have the address at which Mr Horace Lyttleton stayed when in France recently.'

'He moved about a bit: we had three or four different addresses for him altogether. I'll look them up for you.'

Saunders opened a drawer, took out a Boots' Diary, and turned over the pages.

'Here we are,' he said. 'On June 15th, Hotel Mirabeau, Dinard; on June 26th, Hotel de la Victoire, St Malo; on July 7th, Hotel des Bains, Étretat.'

'How long was he away?'

'Let me see—he went away on the 15th of June and returned about the 22nd of July—five weeks altogether.'

When the detective had noted this information, he asked if he could see the office boy, Smith, who was on duty early on the morning of James Lyttleton's disappearance. The manager opened the door and called Smith, a bright-looking though undersized youth of sixteen, into his room.

'This is the boy, Mr Mitchell,' said Saunders. 'Now, Smith, I want you to answer this gentleman's questions.'

'You remember, do you not, the last morning that Mr James Lyttleton came to the office?'

'Yes, sir, it was my early morning.'

'Do you remember someone ringing up on the 'phone and asking to be put through to Mr Lyttleton?

'Yes, sir. Mr Lyttleton had come out just before and told me to connect up to his extension anyone who asked for him.'

'Did you recognise the caller's voice?'

'Not exactly, sir.'

'What do you mean by that?'

'Well, sir, in thinking it over afterwards, it did seem to me that the voice was familiar.'

'Nonsense, Smith,' struck in Saunders; 'no one can recognise a voice on the telephone.'

'It may have been only my fancy, sir.'

'Whose voice did you fancy it was, my boy?' said the sergeant.

'I am not sure, sir, I thought it sounded familiar, that's all.'

'Someone in the office?'

'It may have been, sir.'

'Is that all you can tell me about it?'

'Yes, sir, that is all.'

'You heard some of the things Mr Lyttleton said to the man?'

'I could not help it, sir, he spoke so loudly.'

'What exactly did you hear?'

'Well, sir,' replied the boy slowly, 'I can remember hearing him say "decision, clear out altogether, prosecution."'

'Did he say anything about dissolution?'

'No, sir, I didn't hear that word at all.'

'You told me so, Smith, a few days ago,' said the manager.

'I don't think so, sir, I am sure the word was decision.'

'The boy is a bit muddled, I am afraid,' said Mr Saunders to the detective.

'Thank you, my boy,' said the latter, 'that is all I wanted to ask you.'

'Now, sergeant,' said the manager, as the door closed behind Smith, 'I have something here which I think is of importance.' With this he unlocked a drawer in his desk and drew out a letter which he handed to the detective. 'When Inspector Candlish called here,' continued Saunders, 'he asked what happened to the letters which Mr Lyttleton brought up with him from home the last time he came to the office. I told him I did not know; but yesterday one of the clerks was looking for another document in the chief partner's room, when he found this between the sheets of blotting paper on his desk. He brought it to me; and I should have taken it to Scotland Yard at midday but for your calling here this morning.'

The detective opened and read slowly the following letter:

'HOTEL DE LA VICTOIRE,
'ST MALO,
'29*th June*, 19—

'DEAR JAMES,—I am in receipt of your letter of the 26th and note your refusal to allow me to overdraw my partner-ship account by a further twenty thousand pounds; as you know, I have been very hard hit indeed by the continued slump in Siberian mines, of which I have been carrying over the very large holdings I bought two months ago when the reported "White" victory and the prospect of Japanese intervention made a boom look probable; and unless I can find the above mentioned sum this week as cover, my brokers are threatening to throw the whole of my holdings on the market, when I shall be responsible for losses which will inevitably mean bankruptcy. The matter is vitally urgent, and I must see you privately. I will run over from France tomorrow and will 'phone through to you at the office about 9.15 on the 1st to make an appointment. Don't fail me. Your refusal to help me will mean my ruin. But if I can hold on a few weeks more, the tide is certain to turn, and I shall be able to get out without loss.

'Yours sincerely,
'HORACE LYTTLETON'

'This is a very important document,' said the detective, as he folded the letter carefully and placed it in his breast pocket.

He then took his leave of Mr Saunders and returned to Scotland Yard as fast as a motor bus would take him.

A few minutes later he was closeted with Major Burke, the Assistant Commissioner in charge of the Criminal Investigation Department.

'It looks as though we have got quite a good case against Horace Lyttleton, sir,' he said, as he concluded his report by placing the St Malo letter in his chief's hands.

'We have a good bit of circumstantial evidence,' was the reply; 'and this letter points to a possible motive, but even now it is not clear how Horace would have profited by his cousin's death.'

'He may have hoped to get a free hand in the business and to draw out the money he required to carry over those shares. Success or failure in raising twenty thousand pounds at short notice appears to have meant ruin or wealth to him. Mere anger at having his request refused may have led him to take some desperate step.'

'I admit that things look very black against him, but we have to discover the missing man or his corpse before we can prove either abduction or murder against anyone; and we haven't a scrap of evidence that it was Horace Lyttleton or his son who attacked Chief Inspector Candlish. The next step, I think, is for you to go over to France to get the evidence of the hotel-keepers in whose houses those two gentlemen stayed. In the meantime I'll have them both kept under observation.'

About half an hour later, when Mitchell was clearing up various small outstanding matters before setting off home to pack up his kitbag for his contemplated journey to France, a stolid-looking constable knocked at the door of the Assistant Commissioner's office, and, on being told to enter, said:

'Excuse me, sir, but there's a man come in who demands to see "the head": he won't explain his business to anyone else, and as he says he has information of life and death importance, I thought you ought to know about it.'

'Who is the man?'

'He says his name's Parker, sir, head waiter at the County Hotel, Hillborough.'

'Hillborough,' repeated Major Burke. 'I will certainly see him. Send Sergeant Mitchell to me and show Mr Parker up at the same time.'

When the detective and the waiter had entered the room and been asked to seat themselves, the Assistant Commissioner invited the latter to explain his business.

'Well, sir, it's like this, my name is Parker—William Parker— and I am head waiter at the County Hotel at Hillborough. Not that I'm a native of the place, sir, I wouldn't like you to take me for a countryman, seeing that I was born and bred in Hammersmith.' . . .

'But what is the important business you wish to see me about?'

'I was just coming to that, sir. But first of all I want to ask if you know anything about this matter.' With these words he drew out of his pocket a paper which he unfolded and passed to Major Burke.

'What is this? Oh, yes, the *Weekly Pictorial* for the 6th of July, an article on the "Southshire Mystery"—yes, I know something about it. Have you any information to give?'

'Do you see that picture, sir? Well, I think I can tell you whose it is.'

The picture in question was a woodcut reproduced from a photograph of the face of the man whose body had been found by Inspector Candlish, on the lips of which a moustache had been roughly drawn in ink.

'Yes,' said the Assistant Commissioner eagerly, 'tell me all you know. Who was the man?'

'If I am right, sir, his name was Austin; but how his body came to be found in a stream in Southshire after being buried in the cemetery at Hillborough I can't think.'

'Who was Austin? You had better begin your story at the beginning.'

'Well, sir, Mr Austin was a young gentleman from New Zealand—nice open-handed young fellow he was too.'

(The Assistant Commissioner swore softly to himself at Mr Parker's incurable tendency to stray away from the straight course of his story, but thinking that interference would only make him more verbose than ever, said nothing.)

'Well, early in the year he came over on a trip to see the old country, as he called it, and went to one or two places where some of his ancestors had lived. Now, sir, Mr Austin's grandmother had been a native of one of the villages near Hillborough (Monk's Deighton), so he came to put up at the County Hotel for a few days last May. But, as he took a liking to the place, he stayed on from week to week, and used to go out tramping about the country exploring all the old churches and the like. More than once he said to me, "Parker," he said, "I do enjoy seeing old buildings: in my country everything is brand new, and there is nothing that links us up with the past." Well, sir, Mr Austin had a bad heart, and when he first came to the hotel he asked me for the name of the best doctor in the town. I told him Dr Jennings, who is young and smart, quite different from the generality of doctors we have round about Hillborough— pompous old fogies for the most part they are. Well, sir, one day towards the end of July, poor Mr Austin took a longer walk than usual, and when he got back he fell down on the stairs on his way to his room, and died in a few minutes. Of course, the house being an hotel, the body had to be taken to the mortuary to await burial, and it was while it was there that we had a silly story from Mrs Whiteley, the mortuary keeper's wife, about a ghost; but you gentlemen won't want to be bothered to hear all that, so to cut my story short, Mr Austin was buried in the town cemetery, and Mrs Johnson the landlady of the County Hotel and myself were the only mourners, excepting a solicitor from London who came to represent Mr Austin's family in New Zealand.

'Now, sir, I am just coming to the strange part of my story:

last night, after I had finished my work, I sat down in the still-room to have a few minutes' rest over a glass of stout before going to bed. I had lit my pipe, and was turning over some old papers which I had brought out of the commercial room, when I came upon the bit you have before you. I was reading the account of the inquest and how the doctor said the corpse had been shaved after death, when I thought just in idle curiosity that I would see what the deceased must have looked like before he was shaved; so I got a pen and drew a moustache on the illustration. My word, wasn't I surprised nearly out of my wits to see the face was that of Mr Austin, whose funeral I had myself attended. I jumped up and ran off to Mrs Johnson's parlour, and showed her the picture. She recognised it at once and was in a great state, I can tell you. 'William,' she says, 'off to the police you go first thing in the morning." "Not to the local police, ma'am," says I, "with your permission I'll go up to London to see the head of Scotland Yard. This matter is much too important for the limited intelligence of Inspector Dyson," I says. Mrs Johnson agreed, and arranged for Tom the boots to assist in the coffee room, and here I am, gentlemen.'

'You have told us a very interesting story, Mr Parker,' said Major Burke, 'but I should like to know about the ghost which was supposed to have been seen while Mr Austin's body was at the mortuary awaiting burial.'

The voluble head waiter was only too pleased to have a further opportunity of displaying his eloquence; and he repeated the account of Mrs Whiteley's ghost which he had already given to Chief Inspector Candlish.

'Before you go, Mr Parker, can you tell me the date of Mr Austin's death?'

'The 29th of June, sir.'

'And when was he buried?'

'Three days after, sir, on the 2nd of July.'

The Assistant Commissioner, after thanking and dismissing Mr Parker, rang a bell and despatched a messenger to obtain a

Surrey guide-book. When this arrived, he turned up the map of Hillborough, and having located the mortuary, asked Mitchell for the full address of Mr Horace Lyttleton.

'Holly Lodge, Holly Road, sir,' said the detective, after referring to his note-book.

'If I understand this map rightly, the gardens of some of the houses on one side of Holly Road abut right on to the mortuary grounds. Has any other officer beside Chief Inspector Candlish and yourself been down to Hillborough in connection with the Lyttleton case?'

'No, sir, the Chief Inspector was working alone on the case. Curiously enough, he was also connected with the Southshire case, and I believe visited Hillborough in connection with it.'

'Bring me all the Southshire case papers.'

Sergeant Mitchell left the room, and in a few minutes returned with a bundle of documents, which he handed to his superior officer, who turned them over until he came to the Chief Inspector's report of his visit to Hillborough to endeavour to trace the owner of the collar worn by the dead man. After reading this carefully, he passed it to his subordinate.

'This report appears interesting in the light of the story we have just heard.'

'Do you think there can be a connection between the two, sir?'

'There must be a connection. Just think, the body of a man is found in a stream in Southshire; all clues to his identity have been carefully destroyed, except one which had apparently escaped notice: that one was the almost obliterated imprint of a Hillborough tradesman on the collar; nothing whatever could be learned about the dead man's identity until today, when the waiter from a Hillborough hotel has identified his photograph as that of a visitor at the hotel. Then again, the dates: Austin died on the 29th of June and his funeral took place on the 2nd of July; the body was found by Inspector Candlish on the 6th of July. There is no room for coincidence, sergeant.'

'Have you not been struck, sir, by the further coincidences between this case and the Lyttleton case?'

'What have you in mind?'

'Well, sir, you have just pointed out that both our clues to the identity of the Southshire corpse lead to Hillborough; but in the Lyttleton case, Hillborough is the place of residence of the missing man's cousin and partner, Horace Lyttleton; and, then again, you have just mentioned two dates three days apart— well, it was during those three days that Mr James Lyttleton disappeared. And lastly, as you yourself pointed out, sir, a few moments ago, the grounds of the mortuary, to which we are led in the Southshire case, adjoin the grounds of Holly Lodge, where Mr Horace Lyttleton lives. Now, sir, I venture to suggest that there is only one theory which would explain this whole series of coincidences.'

'Yes, Sergeant, what is it?'

'I'll begin at the beginning, sir, if I may. On the morning of July the 1st, Mr James Lyttleton received a letter followed by a telephone message, both of which caused him considerable annoyance: the letter we know was from Mr Horace Lyttleton, and I think we are justified in assuming that the telephone message was from the same gentleman. We know that later on in the day Mr James went to Hillborough after drawing out of his bank a large sum in notes. Though we have as yet no proof of it, the presumption is very strong that he went there to visit his cousin and partner; for, as far as can be ascertained, he had no other connection with the place, and he had been in communication with his cousin on business of an urgent nature a few hours before he started. Mr Lyttleton arrived at Hillborough Station, and the evidence, I think, justifies us in supposing that he reached Holly Lodge. As no one has set eyes on him since, his cousin or whoever the criminal may have been, must have disposed of his body (either dead or living) somehow; although it is difficult to conceal a dead body, it is much more difficult still to hide a living man for weeks without discovery. The probabilities are therefore that, as a result of the bad feeling which we know subsisted between the cousins, brought to a crisis by the letter Horace had written to James, the latter was killed by the former soon after his arrival at Holly Lodge, that is, some time during the evening of July the 1st. Now the garden of Holly Lodge is divided from the grounds of the borough mortuary by a brick wall; and, on that same night, something occurred which convinced the wife of the mortuary keeper that a coffin lying in the chapel had been disturbed. In the coffin had been placed the body of a young man who had died in the town two days before; and yet that body was found a week later in a stream about fifty miles away. But though Mr Austin's corpse had been removed, it must have been replaced by something, or the loss would have been found out as soon as the bearers attempted to lift the coffin. Now then, we have on the same night within a few yards of each other, a body to be disposed of and an empty coffin to be filled with something which should pass muster for a corpse. I think, sir, the only possible conclusion is that Mr Horace, with the assistance of his son, managed to open the mortuary chapel, unscrew Mr Austin's coffin, remove his body, and replace it with that of Mr James Lyttleton; and I venture to suggest that if the supposed Austin remains are exhumed, we shall solve the problem of the banker's disappearance.'

'Very ingenious, sergeant; but how did Austin's body get down to Southshire? I quite admit the possibility that events took place on some such lines as you suggest, and I shall apply for an exhumation order; but, on the whole, I think that it is most probable that the County Hotel people are mistaken in their identification.'

'If I had been in Horace Lyttleton's place, sir, I should have reasoned something like this: Here is my cousin's dead body: there will certainly be a hue and cry about his disappearance: he is linked to me by numberless connecting threads, and even if he was not observed by anyone on his way down, I shall certainly be one of the people who will come under the notice of the police in their investigations into the case: therefore to attempt to get rid of the corpse by burial in this garden would be exceedingly dangerous; moreover, wherever the body might be taken, it would almost certainly be found and identified; but Mr Austin was a stranger and unknown to many people in England; if his corpse was taken by motor to a distance, it would almost certainly never be identified, because the few individuals who knew him would have all heard of his burial at Hillborough and therefore would never dream that a body found in a Southshire stream could be his; a little superficial disguise achieved by the removal of the moustache would make assurance doubly sure.

'If we suppose that Horace Lyttleton and his son wished to get to Hillborough from France without attracting any unnecessary attention, what more likely than that they should have crossed the Channel and hired a motor-car at one of the ports on this side, telephoned in the morning from the port or somewhere near it, probably Newhaven, or possibly Brighton, which is only a few miles away from it, and at the same time an easy motor run from Hillborough and also from the Southshire Downs. They would have entered Hillborough from the side on which Holly Lodge is situated, where a run through about half a mile of quiet residential streets would bring them to their house without being noticed by anyone who knew them; there is a garage at Holly Lodge where the motor might have been placed out of sight: after the murder, Horace and his son would have waited till after midnight so as to give the Whiteleys time to get off to sleep, then carried James Lyttleton's body over to the mortuary, picked the lock somehow or other, changed the bodies, screwed up the coffin again, taken Austin's corpse to the motor, then off to the Southshire Downs and back to France from Newhaven, after returning the car to the garage from which they hired it. In this way they must have hoped to have destroyed all evidence of the death of James Lyttleton and left his disappearance an insoluble mystery, while creating another equally insoluble mystery if Austin's body should ever be discovered. The only mistake they appear to have made was in carelessly replacing the wreath in the wrong position on the coffin.'

The Assistant Commissioner, who had listened carefully, making an occasional note, with brows puckered in thought, now very deliberately drew a cigarette from a box on his desk, lit it, and then said slowly:

'Your theory appears to hang together, Mitchell, but there are still one or two difficulties; for instance, the telegrams sent to Miss Lyttleton from Euston on the 1st of July, and from Liverpool on the 2nd, and the man who personated her father in New York.'

'The Euston telegram certainly is difficult to explain, sir; if Horace or his son had come up to London specially to send it, they would have quadrupled their risk of being recognised; moreover, one of them would have been away from Holly Lodge when James Lyttleton arrived; for you will remember that he got to Hillborough at 4.50 p.m. and the telegram was despatched at 5.30. If they had arranged for some agent in town to send it off, the whole thing would look like a premeditated murder, of which all the details were worked out in advance; and yet, how could they have foreseen the opportunity of changing bodies at the mortuary?'

'How could they have known of it in any case?'

'They may have taken in a local paper and found a copy of the current number pushed through the letter box when they arrived at the house.'

'That is possible, but what about the Liverpool telegram?'

'Well, sir, there is a train from St Pancras at 2.30 a.m. which reaches Liverpool at 9.12 a.m. If Myles Lyttleton had had a motor cycle, he might have helped his father to load and start the car, and then himself set out along the London road for St Pancras; if he had started at 1.15 he would have had plenty of time to reach that terminus, put his machine in the cloak room, and catch the train for Liverpool. Arriving at the Central Station, he would have had ample time to walk across to Lime Street and to despatch the telegram at 9.40. He then doubtless went to an hotel for breakfast, made necessary purchases of clothes, and finally went on board the *Ruritania*, where he booked a passage under the name of James Lyttleton. After he left the cab at the Central Station in New York I have no doubt that he simply walked through the booking office, waited a few moments to give his cab time to get out of the way, then hired another taxi and drove down to the docks to catch the next steamer for Europe; he may have caught a Compagnie Transatlantique boat direct to Havre, where he rejoined his father.'

'Your theory, sergeant, is sufficiently plausible to decide me to take immediate steps to have the body buried as Austin exhumed. In the meantime you had better go over to France as arranged, and I will have men sent down to keep an eye on Horace Lyttleton and his son.'

CHAPTER XI

'You may bury a secret deep in the earth;
you may seal its grave with heavy stones;
but one day it will emerge from the darkness
and burgeon forth before the eyes of men.'

LAMOND'S *Aphorisms*

Two days later, about half-past eleven in the morning, Basil Dawson emerged from the Tube station at Hampstead, and began the ascent of Heath Street on his way to Long Vistas. The weather was fine—an unusual thing in England—and the hot August sun beat fiercely down on the streets and houses. The discomfort of the hottest day is, however, mitigated in Hampstead by the shade of the trees and the refreshing airs that are nearly always blowing over the heath and the hill.

Basil was enjoying himself—the walk, the brilliant sunshine, and the prospect of meeting Doris, combined to put him into a thoroughly good humour.

Having arrived at Long Vistas, he knocked at the door, and was preparing to throw away his cigarette in anticipation of an invitation to enter, when to his chagrined surprise the maid who opened the door announced that Doris was not at home.

'Miss Lyttleton left this note for you, sir,' said the maid, handing him a letter. 'Won't you come in to read it?'

Basil entered, opened the envelope and read:

'DEAREST,—I am so sorry to miss you, but I have been promised some news of father. I will ring you up as soon as I get back.

'Your loving

'DORIS.'

103

'When did Miss Lyttleton go?' said Basil to the maid.

'About an hour ago, sir.'

'Did she say what time she expected to return?'

'No, sir, you see the motor came up to the door, and when Miss Lyttleton read the note the chauffeur brought, she seemed to be in a great hurry, and only waited to put on her hat and to write to you before going off in the car.'

As Basil made his way back to the Tube station he felt an indefinable premonition of impending evil; an oppression that seemed to darken the day just as a heavy cloud obscuring the sun might have done; but there was nothing he could do but wait and hope that Doris would return safely, and he tried to imagine the delight he would feel when he heard her voice telling him through the telephone the result of her adventure.

Two or three times during the day he telephoned to Long Vistas for news of Doris, but each time to his dismay he was answered by a maid, who could only tell him that Miss Lyttleton had not yet returned. He was not seriously alarmed, however, until the next morning, when on ringing up about nine o'clock he received the same response to his eager queries. Scarcely waiting to swallow a cup of coffee and a piece of toast and butter, he sent for a taxi and drove off to Hampstead as fast as the motor could take him.

At Long Vistas he found the household in a state bordering on panic: the butler Jenkins, a dignified elderly man who resembled an archdeacon in fancy dress (if it is permitted to imagine such a union of the sublime and its opposite), opened the door, and behind him were grouped the subordinate members of the domestic staff.

'I am so glad you've come, sir,' said Jenkins, ushering Basil into a reception room, 'we are terribly anxious about Miss Doris; after her poor father's disappearance, it would be dreadful if she went too.'

'Nonsense, Jenkins, Miss Lyttleton will come back all right,' said Basil, as much to bolster up his own courage by a show of confidence as to comfort Jenkins. 'At the same time, though I am sure there is nothing to be afraid of, I am going to make a few inquiries as a precaution. But I feel certain that any moment may bring a message from Miss Lyttleton.'

'I hope so, indeed, sir,' was the reply; 'and if I can do anything to help in your inquiries, you may rely on me, sir.'

'Thank you, Jenkins. Now, first of all, I would like to see the maid who took in the note which summoned Miss Lyttleton away.'

The butler retired for a moment and returned with a smart, intelligent looking young woman.

'Here she is, sir. Now Thomson, please answer any questions Mr Dawson may ask you.'

'Did you take any particular notice, Thomson, of the chauffeur who brought the letter?'

'All the notice I could, sir; but there was not very much of him to be seen, because he was wearing a great-coat and scarf, and a pair of those coloured goggles that some motorists use.'

'A great-coat and scarf!' said Basil, 'he must have been uncomfortably warm, for yesterday was an unusually hot day.'

'I thought so myself, sir; he seemed to like the sun too, for when I asked him to sit down in the hall while he was waiting, he refused, and said he preferred to stay outside so that he could keep an eye on the car.'

'Then you did not see him with his cap off? What was his voice like?'

'Rough and grumpy, sir.'

'Did you notice the car?'

'Yes, sir. I don't know anything about motors, but when I saw that one, I said to myself that his master must be a bit hard up to have such a shabby looking old car. It looked just like the dingy old things you see labelled "for hire" at the garages.'

'I suppose you can't describe it more fully—did you notice the number or the name of the maker?'

'No, sir, I'm sorry to say I didn't. I only wish I had.'

'What did Miss Lyttleton do with the letter she received?'

'I don't know for certain, sir; but she probably put it into her hand-bag, which she took with her: that is where she always puts letters and bills which have to be attended to.'

'One more question, Thomson. Was it an open car or a closed one?'

'An open one, sir.'

Basil could think of nothing else to ask; so, after trying to reassure Jenkins, and telling him to calm the fears of the female members of the household, he hurried back to his waiting cab and told the driver to take him to New Scotland Yard as quickly as possible.

Arrived at the Yard, he inquired if Inspector Candlish were back; the answer being in the negative, he asked to see some officer with regard to the Lyttleton case—if possible, Sergeant Mitchell. A few minutes afterwards he was ushered into the room of the Assistant Commissioner, to whom he told the story of Doris's disappearance from home.

'There may be nothing wrong,' said he, 'and Miss Lyttleton may return or communicate at any moment; but after what happened to her father, I am, as you may imagine, fearfully anxious; and I felt that you ought to be put in possession of the facts. For Miss Lyttleton's sake, however, I don't want any publicity until we are certain that there has been foul play.'

'I will have inquiries made without delay,' said Major Burke, 'but I think that if no news comes to hand by this time tomorrow, we shall have to assume that Miss Lyttleton has been forcibly abducted; in which case the best way to obtain information will be to court the widest publicity by means of the Press, and by offering a substantial reward. In the meantime, I think it should be a relief to you to know (though this must go no farther) that we are morally certain we know the men who were responsible for the disappearance of Miss Lyttleton's father; and, as they are under close surveillance, it can scarcely be they who are the guilty agents in her case.'

Having arranged to advise the Yard at once if Doris returned home, and to call there on the following morning, Basil took his departure.

After a night divided between his work on the *Daily Gazette* and a few hours in bed, during which fatigue and anxiety fought a long and painful battle for control of his mind, Basil rose much earlier than his wont; and after ascertaining over the telephone that no news of Doris had reached Long Vistas, snatched a few mouthfuls of food and a cup of coffee, and then set off to walk along the Embankment to Scotland Yard.

Having arrived there, he was conducted without delay to the Assistant Commissioner's room.

'Good-morning, Mr Dawson,' said Major Burke, as he rose to shake hands with Basil. 'You have met both these officers before, I think. Sergeant Mitchell is just back from France and Inspector Candlish has returned to duty this morning for the first time since his accident.'

'Delighted to see you about again, Inspector,' said Basil. 'I feared you would be laid up for quite a long time.'

'Thank you, sir, I can assure you that the thought of getting on the track of the rascal who broke my head and nearly finished me altogether, is the best medicine I could take to complete my recovery.'

'Well, Mr Dawson,' said the Assistant Commissioner, when all were seated, 'I am afraid that you have no good news as to Miss Lyttleton's safety.'

'Nothing has been heard of her since she left home two days ago,' was the reply. 'Have your inquiries had any results?'

'I am sorry to say that so far they have not. And what is more, Sergeant Mitchell has just made a discovery which makes it look as though we are not so near solving the mystery of Mr Lyttleton's murder as we hoped we were.'

'Mr Lyttleton's murder!' ejaculated Basil.

'I am afraid there is no doubt that he was murdered, probably on the very day that he left home,' was the reply. 'We have suspected it for some time, but were not certain until his body was exhumed and identified yesterday afternoon—you are astonished, of course, and I think you will be more so when you hear the whole story.'

'Please tell me what you have discovered,' said Basil.

'You will remember,' said Major Burke, opening a folder of papers on the desk in front of him, 'that the last time Mr Lyttleton was seen alive was at the station at Hillborough on the 1st of July. So far as is known, he was acquainted with no one resident in that town except his relative and partner, Mr Horace Lyttleton, who was supposed to be away in France with his son Myles, on holiday, at the time.

'On the 6th of July, Chief Inspector Candlish found in a stream on the Southshire Downs the body of a young man who had apparently died of heart disease about a week before. There was evidence that an attempt had been made to disguise his identity, for the face had been shaved after death, and all marks on his clothing destroyed, except that the collar bore the name, almost obliterated, of a Hillborough tradesman—but I need not elaborate this part of the story, as the papers were all full of what they called the Southshire mystery, and you no doubt followed it at the time.'

Basil nodded.

'It was only four days ago,' continued the official, 'that a waiter at the County Hotel at Hillborough identified the portrait of the Southshire corpse as that of a young man named Austin who had died at the hotel on the 29th of June and had ostensibly been buried on the 2nd of July. Now Austin's body had lain at Hillborough mortuary from the day of his death to the day of the funeral; and it was between those days that Mr Lyttleton disappeared. The grounds of the mortuary adjoin the garden of Mr Horace Lyttleton's house. Now, on the morning of the 2nd of July, the wife of the mortuary keeper noticed that a wreath placed on Austin's coffin had been moved. She thought it was the work of a ghost, and her husband pooh-poohed it altogether, but the point is important. Now if Austin's body had been placed in a coffin at Hillborough mortuary and had been found a few days later in a Southshire stream, it must have been taken out of its coffin either before or after burial; but the Whiteley episode points to the coffin having been disturbed while in the mortuary, during the night of the 1st of July. If Austin's corpse had merely been removed, the undertakers would have discovered that the coffin was empty as soon as they lifted it up on the 2nd. What was in the coffin? Whatever it may have been, its weight was that of a human body. Now a living man, Mr Lyttleton, had been last seen within a short distance of the mortuary, on the very day preceding the Austin funeral. These facts all seemed to point to one conclusion, and arrangements were accordingly made for an exhumation which took place yesterday afternoon: the coffin was found to contain the body of an elderly man; and Mr Menzies, his partner, and Jenkins, the butler from his house at Hampstead, were present and identified the remains as those of Mr Lyttleton. The post-mortem examination has shown death to have resulted from a heavy blow on the temple. An inquest will be held tomorrow morning at Hillborough, and we shall ask for an adjournment after formal evidence has been given.'

'If he was murdered,' said Basil, 'who is the murderer?'

'If you had asked me that question an hour ago,' said Major Burke, 'I should have believed myself in a position to answer you; but now, frankly, I must say that I do not know: as Miss Lyttleton's fiancé, I think you are entitled to the facts that have been unearthed by the officers in charge of the case, but I must pledge you to secrecy for the present at any rate.'

Basil readily gave the required undertaking.

'You will probably have noted two inter-related facts in what I have just been saying, namely: firstly, that Mr Lyttleton was known to be acquainted with only one Hillborough resident, his cousin and partner, Horace; and secondly, that the garden of that gentleman's house was adjacent to the grounds in which the mortuary stands. The house in question, Holly Lodge, was supposed to have been shut up from the middle of June to late in July, during the absence from England of the owner and his son; but Inspector Candlish, when he called there early in August, picked up in the smoking room a copy of *The Times* for the 1st of July: someone must have been in the house therefore on that date, for it was exceedingly unlikely that a fortnight old newspaper would have been brought there after the return of the household. When, in addition to these points, we took into consideration the facts that Mr Horace Lyttleton was on bad terms with his cousin and that his financial position was said to be unsound, we began to suspect that he might have a guilty connection with the case. But this was not all: it was within a mile or so of Holly Lodge, and while Mr Horace and Mr Myles Lyttleton were certainly there, that an attempt was made to murder Chief Inspector Candlish—an attempt for which there could be no motive unless it were to destroy the evidence that he had collected at Hillborough.'

'If this were all, we should have applied for a warrant to arrest both Horace and his son as soon as the fact of Mr Lyttleton's murder had been established; but we were in possession of another piece of evidence which seemed to be absolutely conclusive: a few days ago a letter was found in the late Mr Lyttleton's room at Winchester House, which was addressed to him by his cousin from St Malo on the 29th of June, saying that he was in Queer Street financially, and that he proposed coming over to England, and would telephone at 9.15 on the 1st of July to make an appointment. This letter appeared to explain all the happenings of that fatal morning—Mr Lyttleton's early arrival at the office, his heated interview on the telephone, his departure for Hillborough: a warrant for the arrest of Horace Lyttleton and Myles was applied for yesterday, and here it lies all ready for execution. It will never be executed, however, for Sergeant Mitchell has just returned from France to report that without any question whatever both those gentlemen slept at the Hotel de la Victoire, St Malo, every night between the 26th June and the 6th of July; moreover, on the 1st of July, both of them were present at the table d'hôte lunch and dinner, and both of them played golf at the local links on the afternoon of the first and the morning of the second. On the 7th of July they went to Étretat, where they slept at the Hotel des Bains every night until the 20th, on which day they returned to England— an absolutely flawless alibi.'

'Does Horace admit having written that letter to his cousin?' asked Basil.

'That is one of the first things for you to find out, Candlish,' said the Assistant Commissioner. 'Take all the assistance you need and push forward your inquiries in every possible direction: not a moment must be lost, as Miss Lyttleton may be in serious danger; and I think that when we find her, the men who murdered her father will not be far off. Now Mr Dawson, this matter can no longer be kept private, the Press must be informed, and I would suggest that a considerable reward should be offered for information as to Miss Lyttleton's present whereabouts, and also as to the motor in which she went away and its driver.'

'I agree most certainly,' said Basil, 'and suggest that we begin by offering one thousand pounds.'

'That should certainly bring in some news. By the way, Mr Dawson, don't forget not to mention that you have seen Inspector Candlish.'

Basil assented, and after a description of the clothes Doris was wearing when she left home had been obtained over the telephone from Long Vistas, the meeting broke up.

Within an hour the streets were filled with newsboys rushing along with great bundles of papers, white, green, and pink, while raucous voices and flaring placards proclaimed to the world:

Lyttleton Mystery—Body Found.
Where is Miss Lyttleton?—Foul Play Feared.
£1000 Reward Offered.

CHAPTER XII

'The only intolerable fool is the fool who thinks himself wise: the only unbearable knave is the knave who thinks himself honest. Unfortunately, both are valued at their own estimate by the majority of men and women.'

POCOCK'S *Diary*.

POLICE CONSTABLE HIGGINSON (Z9625) was full of virtues which would have appealed to the heart of the late Samuel Smiles: among religiously-minded people of the mid-Victorian era he would have been known as an 'earnest young man.' He aspired to a detective superintendentship in this world, and to a corresponding dignity in the next: his leisure was accordingly divided between the Bible Class and P.S.A. of the chapel he attended on Sundays, and on week days to the study of such matters as might be expected to advance his mundane interests.

He was a diligent reader of detective fiction, and sometimes, over his last pipe before going to bed, he allowed his mind to form alluring pictures of the day when the name of Higginson would be as famous as that of Lecocq himself. In the meantime, when on night duty, he compared himself with C. Auguste Dupin, who forsook the sunlight for the more chastened and delicate illumination of the moon, and who solved the most extraordinary mysteries during his nocturnal wanderings through the streets of Paris. It must, however, be confessed that our hero did not quite understand the subtleties of Dupin's reasoning, and in practice he preferred the more dramatic methods of Holmes. In his bed-sitting-room in Canonbury he had installed a violin (second hand), a dressing-gown and a hypodermic syringe (this rather as a reminder of his great prototype than for actual use). His landlady, with that brutal indifference to genius which so often characterises such persons, had given him a week's notice to find accommodation elsewhere, when he had first brought home the violin, and she was only induced to withdraw it by his pledge that it should never be used; so it hung in eloquent silence over his mantelpiece.

But with all these spurs to inspiration round him, poor Higginson could not understand why, when he looked at the mud on a passing taxi, he could not at once discern (as Sherlock Holmes most surely would) if the cab had come from Hammersmith or Hackney, Camberwell or Chiswick. But still he hoped; and to force the growth of his feebly budding genius he smoked shag (as Holmes did), and read all the stories of crime detection which he could obtain from the Canonbury branch of Toot's Library.

On the morning of the day on which Doris Lyttleton had left home, P.C. Higginson was posted at the junction of the Hampstead and Euston Roads. It was his duty to hold up the east-west traffic to give free passage to that moving northwards or southwards; and, when that had cleared, to hold the road open for eastward and westward bound vehicles.

Since a well remembered and painful occasion when his sergeant had come upon him unexpectedly in the Euston Road as he was endeavouring to combine the arduous duties of his profession with the practice of induction and deduction *à la* Holmes, and had called him a d— fool and told him to keep awake, Higginson had strenuously resisted all temptations to think while on duty (had not a famous general said to one of his officers, 'Damn it, sir, you're not paid to think,' and were not policemen a sort of soldiers?) But when the driver of a dingy motor-car coming down the Hampstead Road tried to evade the command to stop implied by his raised hand, he could not help noticing when he was taking its number, that the plate at the back had been recently and clumsily repainted: the driver, too, appeared to be an uncouth sort of person, who grumbled rudely at the delay. It was only when the passenger, a very charming young lady, leaned out of the car and apologised for the driver, saying that the journey they were making was of life and death importance, that he refrained from further action and let the car pass.

But he could not help wondering what the urgent business was; why so sweet a lady should have chosen so rough a chauffeur; and why the latter should have been muffled up with unnecessary clothes and goggles on a bright August day.

That night when the labours of the day were over, and he had retreated to the calm and quiet of Canonbury, Higginson doffed his tunic and service boots and attired himself in his dressing-gown. Then, having lighted a pipeful of shag (which he smoked rather as a duty than a pleasure), he cast a longing look at the forbidden fiddle, and settled himself down to enjoy the ingenuities of *The Cask*, by Mr Freeman Crofts. But even that absorbing work could not hold his attention; and his thoughts kept wandering back to the lady in the dingy motor car. At last, laying the book aside, he got out pen and paper and began to write a memorandum of the incident; this did not take long, for his data were scanty: descriptions of the lady, the driver, and the vehicle, a note that on the latter, under the maker's name-plate in front was a smaller plate with the words, 'Young's Garage, Streatham'; a note of the passenger's remark, 'Oh, I do hope we shall not be very long,' and the chauffeur's reply, 'It's not very far, only twelve miles or so'—that was all. 'Sherlock would have built up a whole history on that,' reflected the constable to himself sadly. 'I must read *A Study in Scarlet* over again.'

Two days afterwards, as he sat in the bus on his way from the police station in Tottenham Court Road to Canonbury, he found the front page of the *Evening Sun* covered with flaring headlines and volcanic paragraphs about the latest developments of the Lyttleton case: he read about the muffled chauffeur and the shabby car in which Doris Lyttleton had been abducted from Hampstead. 'Well I am blowed,' thought he, 'my chance at last. Time and all fits in, and I am the only man in London, barring the criminals, who knows where the car came from—I'll teach that old fool of a sergeant to respect me yet.'

With this he jumped up and pulled the cord: the bus stopped and he alighted, only to run across the road and jump on to a bus going in the opposite direction. A change or two brought him to Victoria, where he caught an electric train to Streatham. Young's Garage, he found on inquiry, to be not more than a few hundred yards away and he was soon there.

'Different this from West-End style,' thought he, as he made his way along a badly-lighted gangway between two shops into a grimy shed, the contents of which appeared to be as saturated with oil as is the sardine of commerce. The man in charge, who was attired in a greasy suit of blue overalls, was doing something with a spanner to the interior of a very antique car. On seeing the policeman he looked nervously up (some of us never get over that nervous feeling when we come into contact with the police—it is probably atavistic).

'Good-evening,' said the constable, 'is Mr Young in?'

'No, he went home half an hour ago.'

'Does he live anywhere near?'

'He lives at 99 Redburn Street, Tooting Bec, and you will probably catch him in if you go there at once.'

Having asked for and obtained the necessary directions as to the route, P.C. Higginson presently found himself interviewing Mr Young in his front parlour at Redburn Street.

Mr George Young was a rising tradesman, whose banking account grew more and more satisfactory each year; one of the principles on which he based his conduct and his success, was to mistake always the rank of the people whose favour or custom he sought, and to address them accordingly; many a car had he sold at a good round profit by calling the wife of a stock-broker or other wealthy city man 'my lady,' until reluctantly corrected by the delighted and flattered dame.

During the war he had won the hearts of officers who came to hire, by giving them two good steps in rank. When Lieutenant X received a bill in which he was described as Major, he was unlikely, according to the philosophy of Mr Young, to scrutinise its items too keenly, and to address captains as colonels was, so he said, the surest way to obtain their esteem and their money. So on the present occasion, thinking that the police and other public officials should always be conciliated, he opened up by saying:

'Good-evening, sergeant, take a seat, and tell me what I can do for you.'

'Thank you, sir, I have come to ask you to be so kind as to give me some information about the people who hired one of your cars the other day.'

Now it was not by giving things away that Mr Young had built up his business, so he replied cautiously:

'I am afraid that will be very difficult, seeing the number of people who hire from my garage. But tell me exactly what you want to know.'

'I am making an inquiry as to some parties who were seen driving one of your cars the day before yesterday: do you not keep a list of your hirings, Mr Young?'

'Not exactly that, sergeant, but tell me who it is you represent: is it Scotland Yard or the local police?'

'Neither, in a manner of speaking, it is a matter I am looking into on my own account.'

'Well, I don't see that I should be justified in that case in giving you information about my customers. Anyway, I don't see what I should gain by doing so.'

'What if I said that there was a reward offered for information?' said the policeman.

'Now you are talking a language I can understand. Do I gather that you are likely to get the reward if you get hold of what I know?'

'Maybe I should, maybe not; but look here, sir, I will promise to give you a tenth of whatever I get out of it.'

'A tenth! Why that's not business, sergeant. Come, now, you know something I don't, and I know something you don't. Put our knowledge together and we earn a reward, which we share half and half—that's quite fair and reasonable, I think.'

Higginson did not think it either fair or reasonable, but as he did not know how to get what he wanted without, he was obliged to agree to the terms of the garage proprietor, who produced pen, ink, and paper, and after some argument, two copies of the following agreement were written out and signed by both the parties, each of whom took one of them:

'We agree that if either of us obtains the reward offered in connection with the disappearance of Miss Doris Lyttleton, the said reward shall be equally divided between us.

'(Signed) ANDREW YOUNG.
'GEORGE HIGGINSON.'

Having carefully folded up his copy of the agreement, Mr Young opened a roller top desk which stood in a corner of the room, placed the document in a pigeon hole, and out of another pigeon hole drew a letter which he handed to his new partner.

'This relates to the only car which was out on hire to a stranger the day before yesterday,' he said.

The policeman opened the letter and read as follows:

'THE GABLES,
'WIMBLEDON.
'13th August, 19—

'DEAR SIR,—Your name has been recommended to me by a friend who has done business with you to his entire satisfaction.

'My car has broken down and has gone back to the makers

for repair. In the meantime I am in urgent need of a car for use this morning. I enclose notes for fifty pounds as a deposit, and shall be obliged if you will let my chauffeur have a car, which will be returned in the course of the day

'Yours faithfully,

'HENRY VANDELEUR.'

'MR ANDREW YOUNG,

'STREATHAM.'

'I looked up a telephone directory and found Mr Vandeleur's name there, so I let the car go without any further ado, and about five o'clock that same afternoon, back it came, so I handed the chauffeur an envelope addressed to his employer with forty-two pounds ten shillings in notes, and a receipt for seven pounds ten enclosed. That is all I can tell you about it.'

'Can I see the car?'

'Yes, certainly, I will take you down to the garage, but we'll just have a nip first to keep the night air from chilling our lungs.'

Higginson was not sure what Conan Doyle's hero would have done in the circumstances: he rather suspected that Holmes would have got all the information he wanted without bargaining away half the reward; whether his hero had ever accepted a glass of whisky from a client he could not remember, but his reflections were cut short by his host's—

'Say when, sergeant.'

They drank to each other, and then set out for the garage. 'That is the car,' said its owner proudly, as he pointed to the shabbiest of the half-dozen or so machines which were housed in the shed.

The constable produced a magnifying glass and proceeded to examine wheels, tyres, tonneau, and chassis, but the expression of concentrated wisdom on his face was, it must be confessed, only a mask to cover his entire absence of ideas, and he sighed to think of the unbridgeable gulf that divided his attainments from those of the Baker Street detective.

'The next question is,' said Mr Young, when the scrutiny of the car was completed, 'what are we going to do. It is no use waiting until one of those Scotland Yard fellows noses things out without us. We want that reward, and we've no time to lose.'

'What do you say to taking turns at watching Mr Vandeleur's house?' said the policeman. 'You could be there in the day time, and I would come down to relieve you as soon as I get off duty in the evening.'

'Nonsense, man, what is going to happen to my business if I spend the day mooning about at Wimbledon? No, we must lose no time in going to Scotland Yard and claiming the reward before anyone else has a chance of getting in front of us.'

The excellent sense of this was apparent even to Higginson, whose imagination had been running riot through a jumble of clues, mysteries and marvellous feats of deduction which would lead him by a short cut at once to wealth, fame, and promotion. Reluctantly surrendering these delightful dreams, he assented to his companion's proposal.

'It wouldn't be a bad plan,' said Mr Young, 'if we were to drive up to the Yard now at once in the very car that the young lady was carried off in. It's a bit late, but there's sure to be someone in charge to whom we can tell our story.'

The dingy vehicle was got ready quickly and pushed out through the gangway into the street; and the two adventurers set out to claim the thousand pound reward.

CHAPTER XIII

'The Vicomte de Boisville married a Russian lady: it was an ideal match; for as neither understood a word of the other's language, they could not argue, dispute, nor wrangle; and, even if they had been inclined to quarrel, they would not have known how.'

Memoirs of Madame de Bourguignon

AFTER the break up of the conference in the Assistant Commissioner's room, Inspector Candlish and his assistant walked down the corridor to the office occupied by the former.

'Sit down, Mitchell,' said he, 'and light up. We have got to have a talk so as to straighten things out a bit before we start work.'

The two detectives lighted their pipes.

'You've been through a pretty bad time, sir, I'm afraid,' said the younger.

'Pretty bad, but it might easily have been worse: if the gentleman who attacked me had not been in such a hurry, my dead body might still have been lying at the bottom of that pond, and then my disappearance would have made another nice little mystery for you fellows here to work at.'

'The criminals, whoever they are, are having a long run for their money, sir.'

'Much too long a run, and we've got to stop them before they do any more harm. I do hope nothing has happened to that poor young lady. But our job's to catch them, not to sit here sentimentalising. Now then, the first point is that alibi of Horace and Myles Lyttleton: there is so much circumstantial evidence of their guilt, I cannot help feeling that it is more likely they have somehow or other faked the alibi, than that they are innocent.'

'They certainly are innocent, sir. I took with me to France photographs, specimens of handwriting, and detailed descriptions of both of them: the photographs were at once recognised by the landlord of the hotel at St Malo, by four or five of the servants, by the secretary and a waiter at the Golf Club, and by the man who drove them to the station when they left for Étretat; and all the hotel people were prepared to swear that both father and son had not been away for more than a few hours at a time.'

'Did you think of comparing the paper on which that letter from Horace to his cousin was written with the notepaper supplied at the hotel?'

'It did not correspond at all, but then he might have taken a supply of stationery with him.'

'Did Horace say anything at the hotel about leaving for England on the 30th of June? He may have written the letter and changed his mind at the last moment.'

'He did not say a word. On the 30th of June and the 1st of July both the Lyttletons followed their ordinary programme; that is to say, Myles in a tweed golfing suit, came down to breakfast at 8.30 and set off for the links afterwards, where he stayed until about six in the evening, when he came in to dress for dinner. His father, in a suit of flannels, came down later, and spent the mornings in a deck chair on the hotel verandah, which overlooks the sea front. There he read novels and smoked cigars till lunch time, after which he would stroll over to the Casino. There was no sign whatever that either of the birds contemplated flight.'

'If that is so, then either Horace wrote that letter as a hoax or else he never wrote it at all.'

'It looks to me very much as if the letter was a forgery, sir, but I take it you will question Horace Lyttleton on the point at an early date.'

'I certainly shall. Now if, as looks probable, the letter is a forgery, who forged it?'

'It must have been the same man who murdered James Lyttleton.'

'And banged me on the head,' added Candlish.

'And abducted Miss Lyttleton,' said the sergeant.

'Have you formed any theory, Mitchell?'

'Theories enough, sir, but not one of them will hold water, though it seems to me that we have quite enough facts to narrow down the range of our inquiries.'

'Yes, fire away and say what's in your mind.'

'Well, sir, whoever the man is, he must be someone who knew all about the office and home life of both the Lyttletons.'

'There cannot be an unlimited number of people in that category.'

'Then again, he (or one of them) can drive a car; and moreover, was present in Hillborough on the day you were attacked. Now, why did the criminal try to kill you? Not for the fact that you were known to be a detective working on the case. Of course, there would be police officers at work and if you were put out of the way he must have known that another of us would have taken up your investigations. No, he must have supposed that you had made some discovery of the first importance which would endanger his plans if you were not quickly silenced. He must have witnessed something that very same day which had aroused his alarm—something which gave him the idea that you had got to the heart of the mystery.'

'Wait,' interrupted Candlish, 'you are quite right, Mitchell; he must have seen me talking with Whiteley the mortuary keeper, and knowing, as he did, that the heart of the secret was connected with the mortuary, he must have concluded that I had found out more than in fact I had, and made up his mind to remove me before I had reported my discovery to the Yard.'

'If we are right,' said the sergeant, 'we have got to look for a man who knew all about the Lyttleton affairs and was passing along Hill Road at Hillborough on the afternoon of the August bank holiday just at the time you were talking to Whiteley.'

'It is a pity I have not eyes at the back of my head as well as in the front; but for that little disability we should be able to get right to the bottom of the mystery in just the time it would take me to remember who was passing behind me on that occasion,' said Candlish with a smile.

'Another point, sir, is that our friend must be particularly smart to have so arranged the whole series of events that everything appeared to point directly to the guilt of the Lyttletons.'

'He forgot their alibi, though,' said the Inspector.

'He probably thought that there might be some weakness or ambiguity in the proof of it, in which case the overwhelming circumstantial evidence on the other side would lead to its being discredited.'

'Yes, my boy, and that overwhelming evidence you speak of is so strong that, if anyone but yourself had made the report you brought back from St Malo, I would not have believed him. And now, as tomorrow's work I propose myself to call on Horace Lyttleton at his office in the city to ask him a few questions about that letter, and also to get from him a list of the people who are on visiting terms with him at Holly Lodge. You had better get a similar list from the servants at Miss Lyttleton's house at Hampstead, and then run down to Hillborough, first to see what the servants at Holly Lodge can tell you about the people who call there, and then to see if Whiteley noticed anyone he knew passing down the street while he was talking to me. I'm off home now, as I am still feeling the effects of that bang on the head.'

Chief Inspector Candlish, in choosing a locality in which to live, had in mind three conditions: firstly, he must be within easy access of Scotland Yard; secondly, he must be within a short journey of the country; and thirdly, he must be near a park.

After a good deal of search and inquiry he had, about ten years before the date of this narrative, come to the conclusion that the neighbourhood of Dorset Square came as near to fulfilling his requirements as could possibly be hoped for; and when he took a top maisonette in Upper Gloucester Place, he could travel to the Embankment from Baker Street by Tube in a few minutes, and could quite readily and quickly reach some of the most charming and secluded parts of Buckinghamshire from either Baker Street or Marylebone Stations, both of which were within the throw of a cricket ball from his residence; moreover, Regent's Park with its lawns, trees, and lake was only five minutes' walk from his door.

The Inspector made a point of turning out every fine morning half an hour earlier than necessary, and taking a stroll through Clarence Gate into the park and round the lake. He took with him a bag of stale crusts for the ducks, geese, and swans, and some monkey nuts for the squirrels, who would climb boldly on to his shoulders and even put their inquisitive noses into his pockets in search of the dainties they loved—he did not bother about the sparrows, those Bedouins of the air, who were always on the watch for opportunities of stealing any morsel of food which was left for a moment unguarded by its rightful owner—the sparrows, he often remarked, were most the diligent disciples of the gospel of self help he had ever met with—but this is digressing.

The maisonette at number 101F Upper Gloucester Place consisted of the top floor of a commodious but old-fashioned building which was amply large enough to house in comfort the Chief Inspector, his natural history collection, and his wife.

This lady was about forty years of age, buxom, and, as a rule, good-tempered; her abilities were rather useful than splendid. An excellent housekeeper, she made her own dresses, trimmed her own hats, and kept the flat in order with the occasional assistance of a charwoman. Her spare time, for like all competent persons she had ample leisure, she devoted to district visiting and the charge of a mother's meeting in connection with a local church. Her piety, however, was not excessive: it sufficed to govern her own actions without making her attempt to interfere with the lives of her friends and neighbours. She possessed one supreme virtue in that she did not try to rule the actions of her husband, recognising that liberty and loyalty usually flourish together. Having practically no interests in common, Mr and Mrs Candlish had nothing to quarrel about, and they were regarded by all who knew them as an ideal couple. She had as little sympathy for his hobbies and his theories as he had for her church-going; but each tolerated what they considered eccentricity in the other.

It is only fair to add that they were excellent comrades, and that the attraction which had originally brought them together had, to some extent at any rate, survived the stress of years.

When the Chief Inspector reached home after his talk with Sergeant Mitchell, he was greeted by Mrs Candlish in tones of unwonted asperity:

'This is really too bad of you, Jim. You promised me faithfully that you would only just call at the Yard to report yourself and then come straight home to rest. You know you are not the least fit for work; and yet you have been away the whole day. Why, Dr Jennings was not a bit willing to let you travel up from Hillborough yesterday. You should think of me, dear, before you run such risks.'

'I am so sorry, Mollie, old girl, but there is really no harm done. I feel all the better for getting back into harness again, and as there turned out to be quite a lot of vitally urgent work for me to attend to, I really could not get away any sooner. Besides, I want to get hold of the blackguards who tried to finish my career in that wood.'

'As far as they are concerned, Jim, they are not likely to get worse than I wish them. Why, I can't bear to think of it even now—suppose they had succeeded. I don't think I could have endured to live without you.'

'There, there, Mollie, cheer up, they did not succeed and here I am, as full of life as ever,' said the Inspector, comforting the lady in the manner usual with lovers, even when they are over forty.

When the domestic harmony was at last completely restored, Mrs Candlish insisted on her husband settling down in an easy-chair, telling him to get his slippers on and rest while she completed the preparation of the evening meal.

Two hours later the Inspector and his wife were seated on opposite sides of the table, he immersed in Mr Cherry Kearton's latest bird book; she reading (and perhaps enjoying) the *Church Times*.

A pipe of his favourite mixture and a cup of real coffee made absolutely complete for the great detective the rarely realised bliss which comes to human beings only after they have eaten a perfect dinner, and have no worries—conditions which, alas, are seldom fulfilled.

'You mustn't sit up much longer, Jim,' said his spouse suddenly, looking up from her paper, 'you need all the rest you can get until you are quite strong again.'

'I must own to feeling a bit tired, my dear—what the—?'

It was the telephone bell. In a moment the Inspector was on his feet with the receiver at his ear.

'Yes, who is it? . . . The Yard . . . This is Chief Inspector Candlish . . . (after a pause) . . . waiting there now, are they? Well, don't let them go whatever you do. I will be with you in twenty minutes.'

'My dear,' said the Inspector, putting down the receiver, 'I am so sorry, but I must go; it may be a matter of life and death for that poor Miss Doris Lyttleton, whose disappearance you have heard about. I'll promise faithfully not to be out a moment longer than I must.'

The face of Mrs Candlish had grown longer and longer from the moment she had heard the word 'Yard,' but she was too wise a woman to try to resist the inevitable, and in a moment she was helping the Inspector into his overcoat, saying:

'Take all the care you can, and don't be very late. I shall wait up and there'll be some hot cocoa ready for you when you come in.'

The Inspector was lucky in finding a disengaged taxi in New Street, and he arrived at Scotland Yard well within the twenty minutes he had promised.

He went straight up to his room, switched on the lights, and sent a messenger to the officer who had telephoned to Upper Gloucester Place, asking him to bring up Mr Young and Constable Higginson, whose visit to the Yard was the occasion of his being disturbed.

Sergeant Miller, an officer whose heavy features concealed a shrewd though unoriginal mind, introduced the visitors, and all three were invited to be seated.

On the journey up from Streatham, the ambitious policeman had enjoyed pleasing day dreams in which he pictured himself in the character of a new Sherlock Holmes, enlightening by his insight and genius the darkness of Scotland Yard officialdom; but now that he was brought face to face with the famous Detective Inspector, he felt just like a small boy who has to meet the ordeal of an interview with the head master of his school.

The condescension of the great man in asking him to sit down completed his discomfiture; and when he was invited to repeat the story he had told to Sergeant Miller, after an attempt to adopt a Baker Street pose had ended in a nervous cough, he relapsed into the wooden and mechanical manner in which his brethren invariably give evidence in police courts.

He began: 'I was on duty regulating the traffic at the junction of Hampstead Road and Euston Road at about eleven-thirty on the morning of the 11th of August, when my attention was drawn to a car . . .'

In this way he narrated the events already known to the reader, carrying the story down to the point where Mr Young had admitted knowledge of the hirer of the car.

Anxious as he was to obtain a slice of the reward, P.C. Higginson could not screw up his courage to say anything about it; his partner, however, did not share his modesty.

'Before I put before you the information in my possession, Mr Superintendent,' said he, dealing out promotion to the Chief Inspector with his accustomed generosity, 'I would like to have one point made quite clear.'

'And what is that?'

'I understand that a reward of a thousand pounds has been offered for information leading to the discovery of the present whereabouts of Miss Doris Lyttleton?'

'That is so.'

'Then I take it that the reward will be paid to Constable Higginson and myself if what I am going to tell you enables you to find the young lady.'

'Constable Higginson is doing no less than his duty as a police officer in reporting all he knows to his superiors, but there is no doubt that you would be entitled to a reward if what you have to tell should prove of value.'

Remembering the agreement safely folded away in his pocket, this statement did not have the disturbing effect on the policeman's peace of mind that it would otherwise have had.

'My garage opens at half-past nine,' began Mr Young, 'and when I arrived there on the morning of the day before yesterday I found a man waiting for me. He looked like a gentleman's chauffeur. I thought he must have got a cold from the way he was muffled up.'

'One moment,' said the Chief Inspector, interrupting, 'the constable has just told us that the man he saw in the car was wearing large goggles; he could hardly have been wearing them when he came to you.'

'No, he was not.'

'Well, then, did you get a look at his face?'

'Now you mention it, I am afraid I did not get a really good view of him. You see he had a muffler round his neck, and his cap was pulled down as low as it would go; but the general impression I got was of a youngish man—in the late twenties or early thirties: he was dark and had a black moustache.'

'His own, do you think?'

'Well, Superintendent, I did not pay very much attention to him, as I had no reason to suspect anything wrong.'

'He brought a letter—have you got it with you?'

'Here it is,' said the garage proprietor, passing the document across the table.

'Thank you, Mr Young, now will you continue your story?'

'There is not very much more to tell: the headed notepaper and fifty pounds deposit, together with the fact that Mr Vandeleur's name appeared in the telephone directory, satisfied me that all was O.K., so I let the chauffeur have the car.'

'What time did he start?'

'About ten to ten, I should think.'

'And when was the car returned?'

'About five that evening.'

'I am afraid I shall have to ask you to leave the car here overnight, so that I can have a look at it by daylight. I will send it down to Streatham tomorrow in the course of the day.'

'Certainly, keep it; if it helps me to earn that reward I shall be quite satisfied.'

'Well, then, if the sergeant has taken your names and addresses I won't detain you any longer. Constable Higginson, I shall inform your Divisional Superintendent of your keen and intelligent action. Good-night.'

When the door had closed behind his visitors, Inspector Candlish took up a volume of *Who's Who* and turned up the name Vandeleur, Henry; appended to which he found the following information:

'Born in 1846; educated at Eton and Magdalen College, Oxford; called to the bar in 1869; elected to Parliament for Mapleton, 1873; accepted Chiltern Hundreds two years later; married in 1870 the Hon. Sophia Verinder, daughter of Sir Philip Verinder, Home Secretary, 1860-1865. Author of works on antiquarian subjects, etc., etc., etc.'

'Well, I'm jiggered,' said the Inspector to himself, 'that's a fair facer; that does not read like the description of a man who is given to murder and abduction; but you never know. Anyway, I'll look him up first thing tomorrow. Great Scott,' he continued, pulling out his watch, 'it's past midnight; I shall hear of it from the missus.'

He did.

CHAPTER XIV

'An aristocrat may be disposed of with propriety by the use of the guillotine, or some other humane appliance; but what on earth can we do with his flunkey?'

Revolutionary Letters

WIMBLEDON was not at its best when the Inspector arrived there on the following morning. Although August was not yet out, the air was muggy and moisture laden, and the roads leading up on to the common, so delightful earlier in the year, were muddy and sodden with the rain that had fallen copiously during the night.

'This sort of suburb is well enough in fine weather,' reflected the detective, as he made his way up the hill, 'but for all the year round give me something nearer the centre of things. I like the town well enough, and I like the country better still, but places that are neither one nor the other usually combine the disadvantages of both.'

His philosophising broke off abruptly as he emerged on to the common, which he had to admit to himself was not a bad imitation of the real country, except that one could never get out of sight of houses.

As every one knows, only respectability of the heaviest type (respectability, of course, being measured by wealth) can afford to live in one of the mansions bordering Wimbledon Common. But surrounded as they mostly are by considerable gardens enclosed by high walls, one of them would afford an ideal centre for the operations of a criminal.

Thoughts something like these were drifting through the mind of Inspector Candlish as he caught sight of a man approaching, clad in the well-known blue uniform of the Metropolitan Police.

'Just the man I want,' thought he, as he approached the new-comer.

Introducing himself as an officer of the Criminal Investigation Department, he asked the policeman if he knew a house called The Gables.

'It is about a quarter of a mile off in that direction,' replied the constable, pointing towards Putney Heath.

'What sort of a place is it?'

'Quite a large house, sir; stands well back in its own grounds.'

'Is this your usual beat?'

'It is, sir; I have been on it for six months or more.'

'Were you on duty here about midday on Monday?'

'I was, sir.'

'Did you happen to notice a motor-car arrive at The Gables? It was an open car—old and shabby—the driver was muffled up around the neck and wore goggles, and a young lady in dark gray was sitting in the car.'

'As it happens I did notice such a car, sir. It would have been about half-past one, and I was walking along in the Putney direction, when about a hundred yards this side of The Gables just such a car came up from behind me and stopped a few yards in front. The chauffeur jumped down, lifted the bonnet, and began to tinker with the machinery. When I was passing, he made some remark about the motor wanting a thorough overhauling, and what a nuisance it was being stopped so near his destination. He wasn't a minute or two getting the car going again; and then I saw him drive up to the front door of The Gables.'

'Did you see the young lady?'

'No, sir; she kept her head turned away all the time.'

'Thank you. I'll take your name and number, as your evidence may be of value later on.'

'There is just one other thing, sir.'

'Well, what is that?'

'Just this, sir, that a few minutes after I had passed

The Gables, I fancied that I heard the car come out again and go back on the road towards Wimbledon.'

'You are not sure it was the same car—didn't you see it?'

'No, sir, the road bends round just beyond the house, and the gate is right out of sight fifty yards after passing it.'

'Nothing else you noticed?'

'Nothing, sir.'

'Well, good-morning and thank you.'

'Good-day, sir.'

'There is something very peculiar about that story,' thought the Inspector, as he stepped off northwards. 'If the car was seen in the Euston Road at eleven-thirty, it should have arrived here at twelve or soon after instead of half-past one. I wonder what it was doing on the way. Again, if he was the same man, why should the driver have been so impatient and flurried with Higginson, and here ready, apparently, to invite the notice of a policeman? Well, I shall know more about it when I have seen Mr Vandeleur.'

A circular carriage drive surrounding a well-kept lawn led from the gate of The Gables to the house, which stood about thirty yards back from the road. As he approached it, the detective had to admire—not its beauty, for it had none—but its air of solid comfort, its spaciousness, and its suggestion of wealth.

The door was presently opened by a dignitary in a uniform of restrained and sober magnificence—'coloured livery,' as he used to declare oracularly in the servants' hall, 'is well enough for the households of city people and the "noovoo rish," but the really old families are different'—then shutting his eyes he would lapse for a few seconds into awed silence. One might imagine that during those rapt moments he visioned The Gables as a temple, his employers as its presiding deities, and himself as a sort of high priest.

When Henry Hicks (for this was the hierophant's name) saw the Chief Inspector, he at once classified him as being 'not quite a gentleman,' and proceeded to ask his business with a manner in which hauteur and condescension were judiciously blended.

In no way abashed, the detective produced a visiting card and said that he wished to see Mr Vandeleur.

With frozen courtesy he was invited to a seat in the hall, while Mr Hicks disappeared with the card. A few minutes later he was told that Mr Vandeleur would see him; and he was shown into that gentleman's library—a charming room with lofty windows opening into an old-fashioned garden at the back of the house. The walls lined with books and a number of coin cabinets betokened the literary and antiquarian tastes of their owner.

Mr Vandeleur, a frail, intellectual looking old man, with white hair and a clean-shaven, ascetic face, was seated at a large knee-hole desk in the centre of the room. He held in his hand a strong magnifying glass with which he was trying to read the inscription on a bronze medallion of Pertinax, which he had recently acquired.

But for the social ambitions of his wife, who had all her life aspired—and with some success—to rule despotically over a salon of artists and men of letters, Mr Vandeleur, who was of a studious and retiring nature, would have been perfectly happy in a cottage surrounded with books. But the lady was the stronger character, and so he had to endure the domestic pomp and ceremonial that he hated, and the ministration of the satellites of Henry Hicks, of whom he was secretly in great awe.

'He does not look like a criminal,' thought the Inspector, as he entered the room, 'but, as Bernard Shaw says, "You never can tell."'

'Good-morning, Inspector, pray be seated. May I ask to what circumstances I owe the pleasure of your visit?'

'You have no doubt read in the Press about the disappearance of Miss Doris Lyttleton, whose father was murdered under mysterious circumstances last July,' said the detective deliberately, watching every expression of the man to whom he was talking. 'Well, sir, I have come to ask you if you can assist the authorities in finding Miss Lyttleton.'

With an air of astonished perplexity the old gentleman replied:

'I would be most happy to give all the help in my power, but I am unable to understand what special qualifications on my part have brought you to me rather than to anyone else, seeing that until I read her name in the *Westminster Gazette* last evening, I never so much as heard of the young lady's existence.'

With his eye still fixed on Mr Vandeleur's face, the Inspector held out to him the letter received by Mr Andrew Young.

'May I ask, sir, for what purpose you required that car?'

'Good Heavens, Inspector, what is the meaning of this?' said the old gentleman, after reading the letter twice through and then turning it over as though he expected to find an explanation on the back.

'You should know its meaning seeing that you wrote it,' said the detective sternly.

'But I certainly did not write it, and the contents are absurd,' was the reply. 'My car is not out of order, and is not being sent away for repair.'

'Do you recognise the handwriting and the notepaper?'

Mr Vandeleur opened a drawer and produced a piece of notepaper, which he compared with that on which the letter was written; then he handed both sheets to the Inspector.

'It certainly looks like my paper, and the handwriting is a very fair imitation of mine. There are differences, however, and as I know that I did not write it, I can with perfect confidence pronounce the letter a forgery.'

'We will return to that presently; in the meantime, would you be surprised to hear that the very car in which Miss Lyttleton was abducted, with a lady passenger answering to her description, was seen to enter your gate at about half-past one on Monday last?'

If Mr Vandeleur's amazement was assumed he must have been an excellent actor. In tones of blended vexation and astonishment he replied:

'I should certainly be surprised—surprised and indignant, that anyone should venture to propound so monstrous a fabrication. May I inquire, Inspector, if your visit to ask me these questions is made with the cognisance of your superiors?'

'I can assure you, sir, that my questions are necessary in the interests of justice, and that by assisting me to find the answers to them, you may help to save the life of a young lady who, it is to be feared, is in the power of the assassins of her father.'

'I shall be delighted to aid in any way possible; but the wholly incredible suggestion conveyed in your questions is naturally somewhat staggering to one who is quite in the dark about the whole matter.'

'Let me explain,' said the detective. 'On Monday morning last, a man dressed as a chauffeur, muffled up and possibly disguised, drove up to Miss Lyttleton's house at Hampstead. He handed in a note which there is reason to believe purported to be from someone who promised to give her information as to her father's whereabouts. (We have, as you know, subsequently ascertained that he was murdered on the 1st of July last.) The car was noticed by a constable while it was held up by the traffic along Euston Road. He remembered seeing the name-plate of the garage from which it had been hired; otherwise—as a false number-plate was shown—we might never have been able to trace it. The garage in question is at Streatham, and Mr Young, the proprietor, when questioned, said that the only car he had let out to a stranger on Monday was hired by you, and he produced the letter which you have just read. The statement I made, which naturally surprised you, about the car being seen entering your gates, is literally true, and I would suggest that if you would be so good as to allow me to question your servants in your presence, we might be able to reach a solution of the mystery.'

'Certainly, Inspector, certainly,' said Mr Vandeleur, pressing a bell-push.

Mr Henry Hicks himself condescended to answer the bell.

'Hicks,' said his master, 'will you please reply to any questions this gentleman may ask you.'

Mr Hicks bowed pontifically.

'Can you tell me,' asked the detective, 'which of your fellow servants would have opened the front door to a caller arriving at about half-past one on Monday last?'

'I was on duty myself, sir, at that time.'

'Do you remember a motor-car with a lady in it, which drove up to the door just about then?'

'Quite well, sir; the chauffeur—an inferior person, if I may say so, sir—knocked at the door, and when I opened it, asked if Mrs Ackworth was at home. I replied that no such lady lived here. He then said: "What, this is The Hawthorns, is it not?" I told him it certainly was not. He then apologised for troubling me, and I closed the door. He must have spent some minutes adjusting his motor, for there was a distinct interval before I heard him driving off.'

'Did you notice the lady in the car?'

'I know my place too well, sir, to look at ladies,' said Mr Hicks crushingly; 'and in any case her face was turned away from the house, so I could not have seen it even though I had tried.'

'Have you ever seen the chauffeur before?'

'No, sir, I have not. I have always been in the best service, sir.'

'There was nothing familiar in his voice?'

'No, sir, there was not.'

'Can you suggest, Hicks, how that chauffeur or his friends could have got hold of a sheet of this notepaper?' asked the Inspector, with an appropriate gesture.

'He could not possibly have acquired any of it, sir. No one uses it except the master himself. Mrs Vandeleur,' added the man in reverential tones, 'uses a different paper; and there is still another kind supplied for the use of the household staff.'

'Hicks is perfectly correct about the paper,' interposed Mr Vandeleur, 'the only supply of that paper is here in this drawer, which I keep locked. I cannot imagine how any of it got into the wrong hands.'

When Mr Hicks had been thanked and dismissed, Inspector Candlish turned to Mr Vandeleur.

'You see,' he said, 'what a puzzle I have to solve. As I have no hesitation whatever in accepting your statements, I am forced to the conclusion that there is an elaborate plot framed by the abductors of Miss Lyttleton to screen themselves by making the chain of evidence end at your house. I suppose you can think of nothing likely to throw any light on the problem. For example, do you know anyone who may be familiar with the Lyttletons?'

'Not a soul, Inspector, not a soul. Of course, I have known of the Lyttletons as financial magnates to whom one had sometimes to send applications for foreign bonds and that sort of thing.'

'Excuse me, but have you sent any such communication to them lately?'

'I rather think I have,' said the old gentleman, opening another drawer and bringing out a cheque book, the used counterfoils of which he began to turn over. 'Yes, here it is. I sent them a cheque for £500 on the 15th of last May, with an application for an allotment of £2000 stock in the Ruritanian 7 per cent War Loan.'

'Did you send a letter with the cheque?'

'It is possible, but I really don't remember.'

Having completely failed to find the enlightenment he had hoped for, Inspector Candlish took his leave of Mr Vandeleur, refusing the refreshment which that gentleman courteously pressed upon him. Thoroughly puzzled and disappointed, he made his way back to Wimbledon town, and after a hasty lunch in a café opposite the station, caught a train to Waterloo, and, walking across Hungerford Bridge, arrived at his office in Scotland Yard in a very unenviable frame of mind.

Far from completely recovered from the effects of his recent mishap, he felt tired and dispirited as he entered his room and flung himself into a chair. But a pipe and a cup of strong coffee for which he sent out, soon restored his wonted energy; and, after listening to the report of a subordinate as to the number of letters, telegrams, and 'phone messages coming from all parts of the country from persons who wanted the £1000 reward, he went off downstairs to examine Mr Young's motorcar on the off-chance of finding some clue to the identity of the persons who had used it three days before.

'Have those letters, etcetera, sorted out, Johnson, so that I can glance through the most likely of them when I come back,' he said, as he passed out into the corridor.

The examination of the car proved quite as fruitless as the Inspector's subsequent scrutiny of the letters, and at the end of the day the discovery of the missing Doris seemed to be farther off than ever.

CHAPTER XV

'Let him but look upon his victim's ghost,
And he will cower and cry that all is lost.'
Old Play

THE next morning brought a change for the better in the weather, and a corresponding improvement in the spirits of the Chief Inspector. Hope is one of the three theological virtues, but for all its lofty position in the moral world, it is seldom admitted by the clergy of any church to be dependent, as it unquestionably is, upon such material accidents as a fine day or a good dinner. Whatever the explanation, Candlish, when he arrived at the Yard that morning was feeling buoyant and confident, ready to tackle anything or anybody. He greeted Sergeant Mitchell with a hearty 'good-morning.'

'What luck yesterday, Mitchell?' he asked.

'I am afraid I drew a blank once more, sir. I obtained lists of the people who visit Long Vistas and Holly Lodge, and made what superficial inquiries I could, but there is no one who does not appear to be quite above suspicion. I also saw the mortuary keeper, and tried to stimulate his memory, and all I could get out of him was that he thinks that he saw Mr Horace Lyttleton drive past in his car about the time that you were talking to him.'

'Mr Horace Lyttleton! Why, practically every line of inquiry leads to him and his son. It's lucky for them that they have an absolutely water-tight alibi.'

'They couldn't have abducted Miss Lyttleton in any case, as they were being shadowed up to the time of my return from France.'

'That's true. Well, I must hurry along to see Horace Lyttleton about that letter, but I'd better tell you first what happened yesterday. Hallo, what's that?'

The question was occasioned by the sound of the telephone bell. The Inspector took up the receiver.

'Yes, this is Chief Inspector Candlish speaking. Who are you? ... Mr Burton James ... Oh, yes ... in connection with the Lyttleton case. Well, I can give you five minutes if you will come round at once ... all right.'

'Says he's a friend of Mr Dawson, and has something important to say about the Lyttleton case.'

'Quite right, sir, he came with Mr Dawson to see the Assistant Commissioner while you were laid up.'

'Well, anyway, he is coming on now by taxi, and will be here in a few minutes. In the meanwhile, Mitchell, you had better sit down and listen to me.'

The Inspector then gave a brief account of the appearance of Constable Higginson and the Streatham garage proprietor, and of his own subsequent fruitless visit to Wimbledon.

'If the car passed Euston Road at eleven-thirty and was seen again at Wimbledon at one-thirty, it must have either gone by a very roundabout route or have made a fairly long stop on the way. I should reckon there must be about eighty minutes to be accounted for.'

'When you were speaking, Inspector, one point struck me: the lady in the car was not at all shy of showing herself to Higginson, but she was careful to turn her back to the policeman at Wimbledon, and also to Mr Vandeleur's servant.'

'I had noted the point, which seems to me to indicate that, if the woman Higginson saw was Miss Lyttleton, the woman who was in the car at Wimbledon must have been someone else personating her, and apparently wearing her hat and coat. I think it is pretty safe to assume that the car drove

from Euston Road to an unknown destination—let us call it
A—where Miss Lyttleton alighted, and that a woman ready
waiting at A either took or was given the hat and furs which
had been worn by Miss Lyttleton, entered the car and was
driven to Wimbledon in order to lay a false trail to implicate
Mr Vandeleur, or at any rate to puzzle us.'

'That is just about how I should figure it, sir.'

'I think we may assume, too, that the headquarters of the
criminals and probably the place where Miss Lyttleton is
retained is somewhere on the southern fringe of London. All
the localities in the case are in that direction—Wimbledon,
Streatham, Hillborough.'

'Hillborough—that suggests something. That car might
have travelled to Hillborough and back in the time,' interposed
the sergeant.

'It certainly might.'

At this point Mr Burton James was announced, and was
invited to a seat.

'Don't you go, Mitchell. Mr James, this is a colleague,
Sergeant Mitchell, who is assisting me in connection with
the case you have called about. Now, I am afraid I cannot
spare you many minutes, so will you be good enough to
explain your errand as concisely as possible.'

'I went yesterday to look up my friend, Mr Dawson,' was
the reply, 'and found the poor chap almost off his head with
anxiety about his fiancé. He is not eating enough to keep a
mouse alive, and he can't sleep; he will have a breakdown
for sure, if the young lady is not found soon.'

'I don't think you can sympathise with him more than I
do,' was the Inspector's reply; 'and if you can suggest any
method of search which we have not tried, I shall be most
happy to listen to you.'

'Have a cigar first,' said the American, opening and passing
round his case. He then picked one out for himself, lit it
carefully, and looking at the detective, said slowly:

'You'll find the men you want, or one of them, at Winchester House.'

'What grounds have you for that statement?'

'The men who engineered Mr Lyttleton's murder must have had an inside knowledge of his movements. If it was the same crowd who made the attack on you, they must have known who was conducting the inquiries on behalf of the police—and how could outsiders have got that information? You actually appeared at Lyttleton's offices, and your errand must have been known to, or guessed by, the staff. I am sure that only a partner or an employee of the late Mr James Lyttleton could have carried out his murder and the abduction of his daughter.'

'You can rule the partner out of it, Mr James. Both Mr Horace Lyttleton and his son can prove that they were out of the country in France for six weeks following the fifteenth of June.'

'If that is so, your field of inquiry is still further narrowed. If it was not the partner, it must have been a clerk,' said the American positively.

'I admit the possibility, though I am far from sharing your assurance,' replied the detective.

'Why not put it to the test?'

'In what way?'

'Well, whoever the murderer is, he must be under the impression that you yourself are safely dead and buried. Why not try the effect of exhibiting yourself without warning to each member of the Lyttleton staff in turn, at the same time watching carefully to see how they take it? Ten to one the guilty man will say or do something which will give himself away.'

'The suggestion is worth considering, but it will not be the easiest thing in the world to arrange the interviews.'

'Why not let me go to Horace,' interposed Sergeant

Mitchell, 'and tell him that we want to put a few questions to each member of the staff? I would ask him to let me have the use of a room with two doors for the purpose; you could slip into the room from the corridor and join me as soon as the arrangement was complete, and we were ready to commence operations. In order to prevent those who had passed through the room communicating with the others, we could have them all in a waiting room, usher them in one by one, then out by another door. Of course, the thing would have to be done after office hours.'

'That sounds all right. I think it would be worth trying. You, Mitchell, had better go straight along to the city, see Horace, and tackle him about that letter, and then fix up the scheme you have just proposed for this evening at six o'clock, if possible. Mr James, I am very much obliged for your suggestion. You shall certainly hear the result, which I trust may turn out trumps.'

The American and the detective-sergeant left the great red-brick building together, parting outside to seek their several destinations; and the Chief Inspector settled down to examine another great mass of letters and messages from would-be winners of the £1000 reward.

'Good Lord,' said he, turning over one paper after another, 'she has been identified at Edinburgh, Dover, Bristol, and Cork—all in the same day too. She is evidently no adept at disguises, for these clever people have identified her though dressed up as a policewoman and a Hindu ayah—what a pack of greedy fools . . . Here's another. "It is almost certain that Miss Lyttleton has been captured by Sinn Feiners, and is being held up for ransom in a ruined mill near O'Gradystown in County Roscommon." The people must think we have nothing to do . . . I know what, I will pick out all the letters relating to the counties of Surrey and Kent, including South London, just on the chance that there may be something worth looking at among them.'

No sooner said than done; and presently the Inspector found himself with a selected bundle of about thirty letters which he settled down to read carefully through.

The first informant had seen a young woman answering to the description of the missing lady walking out with a soldier at the Elephant and Castle the previous afternoon.

'D—n it,' said the Inspector, as he flung it aside.

The second, writing from Epsom, had noticed an aeroplane flying over the town in a southward direction on the previous Sunday, and thought it very likely that Miss Lyttleton was being carried away in it.

The third, named Isaacs, asked for an advance payment of 'ten per cent of the reward—say one hundred pounds,' on receipt of which he would communicate what he had to tell.

The fourth had seen a young lady being led away struggling by two policemen in the Old Kent Road three or four days before, and thought she might be Miss Lyttleton, whose absence in that case would be amply accounted for by the seven days' imprisonment for being drunk and disorderly, that usually follows such episodes.

'I wish these infernal people were in blazes,' growled the irate Inspector, 'they have not got the intelligence of a monkey between them . . . Ah, what's this?'

'25 KING DAVID ROAD,
'SUTTON, SURREY.
'14*th August*, 19—

DEAR SIR,—I was riding on my bicycle through Cheam about midday on Monday last when I passed a small, shabby-looking motor-car, similar to that described in your advt. It had apparently broken down for the moment, as the chauffeur appeared to be adjusting some part of the machinery. What made me notice the car was the fact that the young lady passenger seemed to be worrying over the delay, and I heard her say to the man, "Oh, I do hope we shall not be kept waiting long, I am so anxious to get there!"

"'Shan't be many more minutes now, miss," was the reply.

'I trust this information may be of use.

'Yours faithfully,

'HAROLD TOMPKINS.'

'That's more like it . . .'

The Chief Inspector wasted no time in words, but got busy without delay; and within a very few minutes Detective Davidson, a smart youngster recently promoted from the uniform police, was on his way to London Bridge Station *en route* for Sutton.

When he had finished his lunch at the A.B.C. facing the Houses of Parliament, Inspector Candlish took a stroll down Whitehall, enjoying the bright, clear air. 'It is a shame to spoil it with tobacco smoke,' thought he, as he stopped just outside the office of the Paymaster-General to load and light his pipe, 'but I am going to do it all the same.'

At that moment, a man of about thirty, dark, clean-shaven, athletic, and alert in appearance, whose good looks were spoiled, however, by a suggestion of slyness, was emerging from the doorway by which Candlish was standing: he wore a well-cut flannel suit and straw hat, and carried in his hand a banker's leather wallet which was attached to him by a chain passing round his waist.

On seeing the inspector he stopped suddenly, and his face grew first pale and then flushed as though he were under the influence of a strong emotion. By a violent effort he pulled himself together, and passed out on to the pavement behind the detective. He then hastily made his way to the South Eastern Railway Station at Charing Cross, where he entered a telephone box, from which he emerged after speaking for a few minutes in agitated tones.

By such accidents are the aims of justice sometimes defeated, or at least postponed.

CHAPTER XVI

'Few men are nimble-witted enough to lie consistently under cross examination.'

LORD CHANCELLOR LYNCH

HORACE LYTTLETON was sitting in his office at Winchester House signing share certificates, each one of which he finished off with an elaborate and careful flourish. He was dressed with his usual precision. From his monocle to his orchid button-hole, from his watch chain to his white spats, everything was in perfect keeping; and he appeared to be the very incarnation of the successful British financier. The fact is that he was much more prosperous than he had been for some time past. Only the week before the markets had taken a turn in his favour, and the capricious goddess who presides over the Stock Exchange had snatched him out of the bog of bankruptcy in which he was being submerged so recently, and had placed his feet upon the firm rock of a six-figure bank balance.

He felt, therefore, thoroughly pleased with himself and with the world in general. The news of the murder of his cousin, and disappearance of that cousin's daughter caused him a certain amount of annoyance, for he disliked publicity, but it did not touch his heart. There was only one way to do so, and that was through his pocket.

Moreover, with James out of the way, although Mr Menzies was now taking an active share in the direction of the business, he (Horace) was more influential than he used to be. His opinion carried more weight, and he felt with secret pleasure that the manner of the clerks towards him had more of deference than was formerly the case.

Before Fortune had so opportunely smiled on him, much of

his thought and scheming had centred round Doris, by whose marriage to his son he had hoped to restore his position; but now, with the backing of the money he had, and would make, such a marriage was unnecessary; and Myles might aspire to the daughter of one of those needy members of the House of Lords, who prostitute their titles for director's fees.

When Detective-Sergeant Mitchell was announced, Horace, by an effort of will, assumed a mournful expression.

'Ah, sergeant,' he said, 'I do trust you have come to tell me that my poor young relative has been found.'

'I am sorry that I can't say that, sir, but I hope we shall have good news for you in the very near future.'

Mitchell took the chair indicated by a wave of the financier's hand; and as he looked at Horace across his desk, he thought how appropriately a copy of 'Mammon' by G. F. Watts might have been hung on the wall behind him.

'I have been sent from the Yard, sir, to ask for your help in two or three matters. In the first place, will you be good enough to look at this letter.'

Horace took the letter from the detective's hand. As he read it his eyes opened wider and wider, his face became purple, and he fairly spluttered as he said:

'Wh-what the devil's the meaning of this?'

'That is what I am here to find out. The letter was found, so we are informed, in your late partner's room some time after his disappearance.'

'It is an impudent forgery—the rascal who found it must have concocted it for some purpose of his own. How did the police get hold of it?'

'That, sir, I am not at liberty to tell you. I can only say that the letter was discovered under some papers in Mr James Lyttleton's room about two weeks ago. As a matter of fact, the police have come to the conclusion that it was probably a forgery, but they wish to have some assurance on the matter from yourself.'

'You certainly have that. Why, no man of business, even if he was in Queer Street, would ever give himself away on paper, as I am supposed to in that letter.'

'Certain statements as to your financial position are made in the document. May I ask in strict confidence, if they had any foundation of truth? One moment, sir,' added the detective, seeing Horace about to explode with indignation, 'the reason for my question is this: if the statement is not true, then the letter may have been fabricated by anyone who had a specimen of your handwriting to copy; but if true, it could only have been written by a man having some inside knowledge of your affairs.'

'I rely on your pledge of confidence,' replied Horace, 'and will admit that I was financially embarrassed—temporarily, of course—for a few weeks lately.'

'Thank you, sir. Now I am going to ask you if you will let me glance through your staff attendance book.'

The financier looked surprised, but without demur took up a speaking tube and gave the necessary order. The book was brought in and Mitchell took it, and as he turned over its pages made occasional notes.

'Anything more I can do for you, sergeant?' said Horace, when he had finished.

'Could you arrange for the members of your staff to be interviewed one after another by some of our officers? It is thought that one or more of them might be able to give us useful information,' replied the detective, explaining the scheme that he had worked out with the Chief Inspector.

'If you and your colleagues will be here at five to six this evening, I will have everything ready for you,' said Horace, who, since he had seen the forged letter, was only too anxious to be on as friendly terms as possible with the police.

Mitchell took his leave, and at the appointed time returned with a colleague named Barnes. They found Horace Lyttleton waiting for them in the corridor. With a superbly polished silk hat on his head and a large Havannah cigar between his teeth, he more than ever looked the typical modern merchant prince.

'Punctual to the minute, sergeant, I am glad to see,' remarked the financier, with genial condescension. 'Well, I am ready for you. Come in here.'

He opened a door marked 'Private,' and ushered the two officers into a small office with the usual furniture. 'That,' said he, pointing to a door on the right-hand side, 'opens into the general office; you will be able to bring the clerks in one by one, and when you have done with them they could pass out into the corridor, where you could post your colleague to see that they go straight out of the building.'

'That will do admirably,' said Mitchell; then, turning to Barnes, he added in an undertone, 'Slip out and bring the chief up as quickly as you can. My superior officer is coming along in a moment, sir, and I have sent my colleague to show him the way up.'

If the detective had anticipated any dramatic result from the meeting between his chief and Horace Lyttleton, he was doomed to be disappointed, for the latter merely remarked:

'Ah, Inspector, I think I have had the pleasure of meeting you before. Well, gentlemen, I have given Mr Saunders, the manager, full instructions, so I will not wait any longer.'

He then summoned the manager by means of a speaking tube.

'These, Mr Saunders,' said he, as that gentleman entered through the corridor, 'are the officers from Scotland Yard about whom I spoke to you. Please give them any facilities they may ask for. And now, gentlemen, I wish you good-night.'

Mr Saunders, composed, business-like and matter-of-fact as usual, after his principal had shut the door behind him, turned to the detectives, saying, 'Well, gentlemen, and what can I do for you?'

'I noticed from your attendance book this morning,' said Mitchell, 'that four members of the staff failed to sign in and out on Monday last. Their names are J. H. Thompson, W. Billinghurst, F. Saunders, and T. Watson. Did they give satisfactory reasons for their absence?'

'Watson and Billinghurst have been away ill for the last fortnight or so; both of them have sent in doctors' certificates. Thompson was given special leave to attend his mother's funeral, and F. Saunders, my brother by the way, does a good deal of out-door work for the firm, which takes him away from the office. On Monday he was sent to Birmingham to see the brewery people about some matters in connection with the flotation of their new issue of preference shares,' was the manager's reply.

'I noticed, too,' said Mitchell, 'that several members of your staff were away during the first week in July. I suppose they were on holiday.'

'July, August, and September are slack months in the city, and there is not a week in them during which several of our people are not away.'

'I see that your brother and Mr Billinghurst were absent then. Were they on holiday?'

'It is very probable, but I cannot give you exact details from memory.'

'Do you know anyone living at or near Cheam in Surrey?' suddenly interposed the Chief Inspector, throwing himself forward, and looking Saunders straight in the eye.

'No, I do not,' was the reply that came after a fraction of a moment's hesitation.

'You seem to be not quite sure about it, Mr Saunders; think now, the question is of great importance.'

The manager with perfect self-possession replied:

'The reason for my hesitation was that the name and place were familiar to me once, as an uncle of mine lived there up to his death two or three years ago.'

'But you know no one there now?'

'No one.'

'What is the name of the clerk who found that letter from Mr Horace Lyttleton to Mr James, which you handed to my colleague Mitchell a little time ago?'

'Oh, that was Davis, one of the office boys.'

'By the way, are the whole of your staff here now?'

'All except the two men who are, as I told you, away ill.'

'Thank you, Mr Saunders, and now, if you will be so kind as to let me know your home address in case I may have to communicate with you out of office hours, I will not detain you longer.'

'Here is my card. Good-night, gentlemen, I shall be glad to assist you at any time,' said the manager, as he took his departure.

The clerks were then called in one by one in order of seniority, and each was requested to furnish his name and address, each one was asked when he had had his holidays and where he had spent them, and on each was sprung a question as to whether he knew anyone living at or near Cheam. The Chief Inspector did the talking while Sergeant Mitchell made notes of the replies of the staff. Barnes patrolled outside in the corridor as arranged.

Special care was taken by Candlish when interviewing Messrs J. W. Thompson and F. Saunders, the two men who had been absent from the office on the day of Doris Lyttleton's abduction. The former was a tall, fair, sturdily-built young man of about twenty-five, with a toothbrush moustache, who looked as though his strength lay rather in his biceps than in his brain.

Having stated his address to be 91 Downs Road, Sutton, he was asked the usual question about Cheam.

'Oh, yes,' he replied, 'I know several people there. In fact I lived there all my life until my people moved into Sutton last year.'

'What was your address at Cheam?'

'The Willows, Dene Road.'

'Can you drive a motor?'

'Yes, I was in the A.S.C. during the war, and used to drive a lorry; but I haven't had much practice since.'

'Have you driven a car recently?'

'That is a funny question, isn't it? Well, no, I have not; but if the chance came my way, you bet I'd take it without asking the police for permission.'

'If you were caught driving a car without a licence, you would be liable to a thumping fine,' said the Inspector magisterially.

'Oh, I have got a licence all right,' said the clerk. 'It is worth sporting five bob for the chance of getting a spin now and again, when funds run to it.'

'Have you ever hired a car from Young's garage at Streatham?'

'Never even heard of it.'

'Have you ever been in Dublin?'

'No.'

'Or in Paris?'

'Yes, for a few days last year.'

'Or in New York?' (This question came suddenly and swift as a pistol shot.)

'New York . . . n-no.'

'Why do you hesitate?'

'Because I have been pretty near it at Halifax, Nova Scotia.'

'When was that?'

'When I was a kid.'

Mr Frederick Saunders was in appearance like his brother, only several years younger. There was more of the flexibility of youth about him, and his face was still something of a mask to his emotions, which had not yet stamped their mark permanently on his features, as they do during the years between forty and sixty. He had a good deal of his brother's ability, and was looked on by his fellows as destined to a high position in the service of Lyttletons.

He informed his questioner that he shared a house with his brother at 3 Haselden Road, Purley, near Croydon.

'Where were you on Monday last?'

'In Birmingham for the firm.'

'You do a good deal of outdoor work?'

'Yes, a good bit.'

'Do you know anyone living in or near Cheam?' came the next question suddenly.

'Ye—that is, no—no one.'

'You hesitate; are you not sure?'

'Quite sure, I was thinking of something else for the moment.'

'Did you ever know anyone at Cheam?'

Saunders thought for an appreciable interval before replying 'no.'

'But your brother said that your uncle used to live there.'

'Oh, yes, of course; stupid of me, Inspector, but I thought you were referring to someone outside the family.'

'What was your late uncle's address?'

'Haydock's Farm, near Cheam,' came the reply slowly.

'Do you hold a motor driver's licence?'

'No.'

'Can you drive?'

'A little.'

'When did you drive a car last?'

'Oh—let me see—I think it must have been during my holidays last year.'

'Ever heard of Young's garage at Streatham?'

'Young's garage at Streatham,' came the answer slowly. 'No, I have never heard of it.'

'Where did you spend your holidays last July?'

'At home. I was feeling off colour, and I thought a good rest would do me more good than the fuss of a sea-side boarding house.'

'Ever been to New York?'

'To New York?' repeated the clerk—'whatever makes you think I have been there?'

'Have you?'

'No, certainly not. I have never been farther west than Torquay.'

The last of the office staff to come before the detectives was Davis, the boy who had found the letter in the late senior partner's room.

'Do you remember, Davis, being sent to look for a paper in the late Mr James Lyttleton's room, about two or three weeks ago?'

'Do you mean, sir, the time when I found that letter between the sheets of blotting paper on his desk?'

'Yes, that is what I want to know about. Now, first of all, what were you sent to look for?'

'A letter from Glyn Mills' Bank, sir.'

'Who sent you?'

'Mr Saunders, sir.'

'Did you find the letter?'

'No, sir, the other boy, Smith, found it afterwards in one of the letter baskets waiting to be filed.'

'How long had it been there?'

'Not long, sir, because we have to clear those baskets out every morning, and file the letters.'

'Did Mr Saunders tell you where to look?'

'He only told me to turn over every scrap of paper on the desk until I found the letter, sir.'

'Why did you take the other paper to him when it was not about what you were told to look for?'

'Because I thought it was funny that it should have been hidden away like that—and besides, sir—'

'Well, my boy, what is it?'

'I thought it might be a clue.'

'Ah, you have been reading detective stories, have you?'

'Yes, sir, I always read the Sexton Blake books.'

'I expect you find real detectives very ordinary and uninteresting after Sexton Blake, eh, Davis?'

The boy's looks spelt assent, though he was too polite to say more than, 'Oh, no, sir.'

Davis having been dismissed, the detectives gathered up their papers and took their departure, leaving the offices to the caretaker, who had for the last hour been hanging about the corridor, waiting for them to go, so that he could set his satellite charwomen to work on their nightly task of cleaning, scrubbing, and polishing furniture, floors, and door-handles to that pitch of perfection which is considered befitting to such a temple of the high finance as the office of Lyttleton, Menzies, and Lyttleton.

CHAPTER XVII

'Every yard farther from the starting point is that much nearer
the end of the journey.'

'Now, BARNES,' said the Chief Inspector, as the three C.I.D,
men stood on the pavement of Old Bond Street, 'you can cut
along home. Mitchell,' he added, after Barnes had stepped off
in the direction of the Bank tube station, 'you and I have got a
lot to talk about; and as I, for one, can't think on an empty
stomach, we will go to get a bit of dinner first. I told my wife
I should probably be late. I know a little place within a stone's
throw of this, where we can get good grub, and what is more,
the tables are not so close together that everything one says can
be overheard.'

To give the exact address of Burdett's Restaurant would be
to let loose upon it an embarrassing rush of new customers,
altogether in excess of its seating accommodation. Suffice it to
say that it is situated in a busy side turning not far from Liverpool
Street Station. One enters from the street into a narrow room,
down one side of which is a bar with a high counter, at which
during the lunch hour clerks from the neighbouring banks and
offices sit on stools and consume large plates of solid old-
fashioned fare, such as roast beef, steak pudding, or Irish stew,
washed down by draughts of ale or stout direct from what
Dickens so appropriately called 'its native pewter.' Behind the
backs of the gentlemen who sit at the bar is a narrow passage,
from which at the farther end of the room a staircase leads to
the first floor, while the passage itself swerves round to the left
into a back dining-room.

At midday, of course, all the rooms on both floors are

crowded, but in the evening the attendance is much less numerous, and one can be sure of getting a table to oneself.

'At so many of these places,' said Candlish, as he and his assistant seated themselves at a cosy corner table in the back room, 'where there isn't much evening trade, they warm up what is left of the midday stuff; but this is an exception.

'Good-evening, Henry,' said he to the waiter, a greasy but genial individual who bustled up, gave the table three or four flicks with a serviette, and held out a menu. 'What can you really recommend this evening?'

'Good-evening, sir, don't often have the pleasure of seeing you here nowadays,' replied the waiter, who continued, 'There's a beautiful boiled neck of mutton in cut, sir, or if you prefer it, the steak toad-in-the-hole is first-rate tonight.'

A minute afterwards the voice of Henry might have been heard bawling enigmatically down the service lift—'Boiled neck cut lean, turnips and boiled, once; steak toad, cabbage and baked, once.'

Dinner over, with cups of coffee in front of them, and pipes well alight, Candlish and Mitchell settled down to discuss their evening's work.

'That American chap's idea that one or more of them would think they saw a ghost when they looked at me, didn't come off, Mitchell.'

'It would have made things easy for us if they had; but the fact that no one looked startled at the sight of you does not by itself prove that all the men we saw this evening were innocent. You have been out and about for the last two or three days, and you may have been seen by one of the guilty parties.'

'Not impossible, Mitchell; I agree with you there.'

'It seemed to me, sir, that several of them appeared to be a bit uneasy.'

'Not more so than a nervous man might be if unexpectedly asked a lot of questions by detectives. He might be as innocent as a new-born babe, and yet be afraid of being suspected. But let us go through your notes.'

The entries about each clerk had been made on a separate sheet of paper. Candlish took out his fountain pen, and numbered each consecutively; there were forty-five in all.

'Now,' he said, 'I am going first to read out the numbers of all those who live in South London or Surrey. Take them down as I call them out.

'How many have you got?' said he, when he had finished.

'Eighteen.'

'Very well; now for the numbers of those who admitted a knowledge of Cheam. How many is that?'

'Four.'

'Now for those who confessed to a knowledge of motor driving.'

'Six that time, sir.'

'And those who were away on holiday during the first week in July?'

'Eight,' said Mitchell, when the Inspector had finished dictating.

'And those away last Monday—17, 21, 34, 39—four in all. Now then, Mitchell, how many numbers appear in all your five lists?'

'Two only, 21 and 39.'

'Let me see, 21 is Saunders Junior, and 39 is Thompson—we must look those two gentlemen up. I didn't much like the way either of them answered my questions this evening. You had better go straight down to Purley in the morning, and make some inquiries about the household at No. 3 Haselden Road; especially find out, if you can, whether the younger Saunders was seen about during the first half of July, when he says he was at home on holiday; and then see if you can find out anything about young Thompson at Sutton, and ascertain if his mother really was buried last Monday.

'There's a tram, I believe, from Croydon to Sutton, which

will help you; you had better 'phone me at the Yard between twelve and one to report progress.'

About half an hour later, after the Chief Inspector had been duly scolded by his spouse for working so much harder and longer than an invalid should, he replied:

'Never mind, my dear, I really think I am beginning to see daylight in the Lyttleton case at last, and when that is done with, I will arrange to take the week still due of my annual leave, when I will rest enough to satisfy even you.'

Promptly at nine-thirty on the following morning, Detective Davidson presented himself in Candlish's room to report.

'I went straight down to Sutton, sir, and called at No. 25 King David Road, where I saw Mrs Tompkins, who stated that her husband was at work in the city and would not be home till seven p.m. When I explained my business, she said that she had been cycling with her husband when he saw the car, and would be quite willing to accompany me to Cheam to point out the exact spot. Having arrived at Cheam, she took me through the village to a point just outside a butcher's shop, where the car had been standing when she and her husband had passed it. It was, she said, apparently going in the direction of Ewell.

'As far as I can judge from a map which I bought at Sutton, no one coming from town would use the road through Cheam if they wanted to go beyond Ewell, as there is a more direct route from London to the latter town. I gathered, therefore, that in all probability the destination of the car was somewhere on the main road between Cheam and Ewell, perhaps down a side road leaving the highway on the Cheam side of Ewell.

'I questioned the butcher and his assistant, and the tenants of the adjacent shops, but could obtain no further information. I also called on the local police, who had already been making inquiries at the request of the Yard, but they had nothing to tell me.'

'Very good indeed, Davidson. Now I want you and Barnes

to go straight down to Cheam, get in touch with the local police, and then beat up the country between Cheam and Ewell to see if you can hear anything more about that car. At the same time, make inquiries at Cheam about a man named Thompson who formerly resided at a house called The Willows, Dene Road. And you might also see if you can find out anything about an old gentleman named Saunders, who used to live somewhere in the neighbourhood, at a place called Haydock's Farm. As tomorrow is Sunday, you and Barnes had better put up at Cheam over the weekend, and report progress to me by 'phone (Paddington 19763) at 6 p.m. tonight, and at the same time tomorrow. The matter is very urgent, so don't waste any time.'

Having dismissed Davidson, Inspector Candlish stepped across to the office of his chief, Major Burke, and gave that gentleman a very full account of the work that had been done up to date on the Lyttleton case.

'I rather think we shall be near a solution of the mystery when we get reports from Mitchell, Davidson, and Barnes,' said he.

There followed a conversation, in the course of which Candlish and his Chief weighed all the possibilities of the case, and made plans to meet the most probable contingencies.

'There is just one other point, Candlish,' said the Assistant Commissioner, as the Inspector was about to rise, 'I have been thinking about that telegram which purported to have been despatched from Euston by James Lyttleton to his daughter on the day of his disappearance.'

'I remember quite well: we made inquiries at the time. The original was in printed letters, and none of the clerks at the Euston telegraph office could remember anything about the messenger who brought it, which is natural, considering the enormous number of people who use the office, and the fact that some weeks had elapsed before the inquiries were made.'

'In the light of what you have just been telling me, don't you think it possible that the missing messenger may have been one of the office boys at Lyttleton's?'

'Quite worth looking into, sir. I'll run down to the city now— there will just be time before the office closes at one o'clock for the Saturday half-holiday.'

At three minutes to one, Candlish was standing on the east pavement of Old Broad Street opposite Winchester House. 'The chances are,' thought he, 'that the clerks will all be out by two minutes after the hour. They don't hang about unnecessarily in the city on Saturdays. The two boys will probably be a few minutes later, as they have the letters to copy and get ready for post.'

His surmise was right, and there was an appreciable interval after the dispersal in various directions of their seniors, before the two boys, Smith and Davis, made their appearance, each carrying a bundle of letters.

Candlish moved on a few steps, and then turned and walked back, timing himself to meet the boys as they crossed the road.

'Hallo,' he said, 'aren't you the two young gentlemen I saw yesterday?'

'Yes, sir,' came the reply in a duet.

'Finished for the day?'

'Yes, sir.'

'And going home to dinner, I suppose?'

The boys assented.

'What do you say to some lemonade and an ice before you start?'

Only one answer to such a question has ever been given by boys, and Smith and Davis were no exceptions to the general rule. So after posting the letters they followed the detective into a little Italian grub-shop close to Broad Street Station, where they were quickly engaged in the consumption of large pink and yellow ice creams, an occupation which, judging by the rapt expression of their faces, afforded them considerable satisfaction.

'How far off do you boys live?' asked Candlish genially.

'I live at Walthamstow, sir,' said Smith.

'And I at Watford, sir,' remarked his youthful colleague.

'Then you go from Liverpool Street, Smith; and you, Davis, from Euston. Is that it?'

'Yes, sir,' came the duet.

'I suppose you know Euston Station well, Davis?'

'Pretty well, sir.'

'Whereabouts is the telegraph office?'

'Quite close to the main booking hall, sir.'

'When were you in there last?'

'I went in there to send off a telegram for Mr Lyttleton about two months ago.'

'Those ices all right—do you think you could manage some more? Ah, I thought you could. Here, waiter, bring two more of those mixed ices,' said the Inspector. 'Let me see, now,' he continued, when the boys had shyly murmured their thanks, 'you were telling me about the telegraph office at Euston. Was it Mr James or Mr Horace that gave you that telegram to despatch?'

'It was for Mr James Lyttleton, sir, though he didn't give it to me himself.'

'Oh, how was that?'

'Well, sir, it was the last day Mr Lyttleton came to the office. I remember, because it was my birthday. Some of them got to know about it at the office, and about a quarter-past three o'clock, Mr Saunders, the manager, rang for me to go into his room. He said he had heard something about it being my birthday, and asked me if I would like to go home early. I said "Thank you very much, sir," and then he gave me a telegram and said that Mr Lyttleton wanted it sent off, and that I had better despatch it from the station at Euston on my way home.'

'But I think I remember that the time of despatch on the telegram was half-past five. How was that, if you left the office at a quarter-past three?' The boy looked uncomfortable, and his cheeks grew red.

'All right, my boy,' said Candlish in a fatherly tone, 'no harm will come to you if you tell me just what happened.'

'Well, sir, as it was my birthday, I had one or two presents in money, and I thought I would like to see the pictures on the way home, so I went into the "Cinemapallis" in Euston Road, and forgot the telegram. When I came out, I remembered it all of a sudden and ran down to the station to send it off.'

'How was it you did not say anything to anyone, when you read in the papers that Mr Lyttleton had never gone to Liverpool after all?'

'Well, sir, I was afraid at first that I should get into a row for forgetting to send off the telegram till so late; but afterwards I made up my mind to tell Mr Saunders.'

'What did he say?'

'He told me it was very wrong of me to have forgotten what I was told to do; but he said it did not matter, and I had better not say any more about it to anyone, as I should only get myself into trouble without doing anyone any good.'

'You are quite sure it was Mr Saunders and not Mr Lyttleton who gave you the telegram?'

'Oh, yes, sir, quite sure. It was soon after Mr Lyttleton had gone off in the taxi he sent Smith to fetch, and Mr Saunders was just going out himself. He had his hat on when he was speaking to me. I remember it all quite well, sir.'

'Thank you, my boy. What you have told me may be of great use. Now then, have some buns and ginger beer to finish up with. What do you say, Smith?'

The last vestige of trouble vanished from Davis's face at the sound of his favourite summer beverage, and it was a pair of thoroughly contented youngsters who parted from the Inspector outside the café a few minutes later.

'I have been hearing the name Saunders pretty often during the last day or so,' thought Candlish, as he walked down the steps leading to the platform of Liverpool Street Metropolitan Station *en route* for Baker Street. 'No chance of any botanising this afternoon,' he added, glancing up at the clock. 'I shall not get my lunch before half-past two, and I must be in at six in case those fellows in Surrey have anything to report.'

CHAPTER XVIII

'They sight the foe; they prick their steeds:
They prime themselves for gallant deeds:
The chieftain shouts, "On, Scotland, on:
The charge is launched: the day is won."'
                                    Border Ballads

BASIL DAWSON was going through days and nights of mental torture, for suspense is harder to bear than ruin, and doubt is worse than death itself.

Work was his only anodyne, and the hours that he spent each evening on the preparation of his column of criticism and comment at the *Daily Gazette* office brought him the only relief that he enjoyed at all during that black week.

He had in sheer restlessness journeyed to Hampstead several times, and was constantly telephoning for news to Scotland Yard and to Long Vistas; and each failure to obtain it brought his anxiety nearer to absolute despair.

It was Saturday evening, and having no work to distract his mind, he was sitting in his chambers, brooding and smoking cigarette after cigarette, when a resounding double knock on his front door preluded the entry of Burton James.

'I have just come from Scotland Yard, Dawson,' said he in rapid tones. 'I looked in to see if they had any news of Miss Lyttleton, and Candlish sent down a message asking me to fetch you along at once. They have got hold of something at last.'

'Good God, man,' shouted Basil, springing to his feet and clutching his friend by the arm. 'Is she safe? Speak!'

'I hope so; I believe so; but I don't know. Come on quickly and we shall find out.'

Basil seized his hat, and the two friends tore down the stairs and out into Fleet Street, whence a taxi whirled them in a few minutes to Scotland Yard.

As soon as they had given their names they were taken up to the Chief Inspector's room, where they found that officer with his assistant, Sergeant Mitchell. Both were standing hat in hand.

'For God's sake,' said Basil, as soon as he caught sight of the Inspector, 'tell me, is Miss Lyttleton safe?'

'I have every reason to think so,' was the reply. 'We have discovered where she was taken to, and we are going down now to rescue her. I take it that both you gentlemen would like to come with us?'

Basil and the American eagerly assented.

'I am equipped for a scrap, if there is going to be any rough-house business,' remarked the latter grimly, as he touched something hard which reposed in his hip pocket.

'You must pledge yourself, Mr James, not to pull that revolver out without my permission,' said Candlish.

'Right you are,' was the reply.

'Now then, gentlemen, my story must keep till later on. I have a motor waiting, so come along.'

'Where are we going?' asked Basil, as they descended the stairs.

'Surrey,' was the laconic reply.

The car proved to be a large Daimler. Detective-Constable Pendleton, a powerfully built man in plain clothes, was seated in front by the side of the driver, and Candlish, Mitchell, Burton James, and Basil Dawson packed themselves in behind.

It was about 7.30 p.m. 'summer time' when they started, and dusk was already beginning to fall.

The driver knew his job, and before they were well across Westminster Bridge, the car was making a fair speed. Lambeth, Stockwell, Clapham, Balham, and Streatham were left behind in turn, and they soon arrived at Sutton, where the car turned off towards Cheam and Ewell.

It was quite dark when they reached the former of these, and in response to a word from the Inspector the car slowed down and stopped opposite the railway station. A man rode up on a bicycle.

'That you, Davidson?'

'Yes, sir,' was the reply.

'How much farther have we to go?'

'About a mile and a half along the high road, and then a few hundred yards down a side turning.'

'Well, you had better pedal along in front to show us the way. Drive slowly about a hundred yards behind him, Smith,' said Candlish to the chauffeur in a half whisper.

It was a heavy, dark, oppressive night, with 'thunder in the air.' In the car, too, the psychic atmosphere was electric. The excitement of the occasion and suspense as to its issue held each member of the party in a state of tense, almost breathless, silence. Basil could see the red tail-light of the bicycle in front. He seemed to have felt so much that he had got beyond feeling altogether. He was like a man in a dream; the car, his companions, the lights—all were fantastic and unreal; the night with its tangible blackness lay like a pall upon his heart. It alone appeared living, inimical and fraught with menace.

In a few minutes he was brought back to the normal by the slowing down of the car, which turned round into a narrow lane, scarcely more than a cart track. Then the vehicle came to a stop, and the Inspector alighted and held a brief conversation in undertones with Davidson.

'Now,' said he to the occupants of the car, 'we are going to do the rest of our journey on foot, and if you will all alight, except Smith, who will stay to look after the motor and the cycles, I will explain in a few words what we are going to do. But first of all let's have those lights covered up.'

When this had been done and the members of the expedition had grouped themselves round him, he said:

'Now, Davidson, you have explored the ground, just describe exactly the lay of it.'

'The house is about three or four hundred yards down the lane, sir,' said that officer in reply. 'There are no other dwellings near it; it stands about fifty yards back and is approached by a path leading through a badly-kept vegetable garden. The path runs up to the front door, and then bends round to the back of the house, where there is a yard surrounded by old farm buildings. There is a dog chained up in the yard close to the back door. I left Barnes on the watch in a field opposite the house.'

'Then you had better go ahead and find him: we will follow you slowly down the lane.'

Davidson left them, walking quickly into the darkness, and the rest of the party followed slowly in the same direction.

'We had better march in single file,' whispered Candlish. 'I have an electric torch, but I am not going to use it unless I must, as the flash might be seen from the house.'

The party groped their way along the lane, the surface of which was rough and uneven. One or other of them was constantly stumbling. Short as it was, the way seemed interminable, and the impression of unreality descended again upon Basil's mind.

At last footsteps were heard approaching from the opposite direction, and in a minute they heard the Inspector murmur:

'That you, Davidson?'

'Yes, sir, and Barnes is here with me.'

The party closed up round their leader.

'Now, Barnes, has anyone been in or out of the house since the two men went in early in the evening?'

'Not by the lane, sir,' was the reply.

'Have you seen any signs of life?'

'Yes, sir, there are lights in two windows on the ground floor, on the right of the front door and also over the fanlight.'

Candlish paused for a moment in thought.

'You say the front door is directly opposite the gate?'

'Yes, sir,' answered Barnes, 'the path from the one to the other runs in a straight line.'

'All right, then this will be our plan of campaign. Mitchell, you, with Barnes and Pendleton, will go on in front of the rest of us, and make your way round to the back door as quietly and quickly as possible. If the dog barks, you must make a rush for it, and if he attacks you, shoot him. The rest of the party will follow me to the front door, at which we shall knock after allowing Mitchell and his assistants time to get to their posts in the rear.

'As soon as you, Mitchell, hear the row beginning in front, you must knock at the back door, and if you hear me whistle twice, force it. The men we are after will be pretty desperate and may resist. Now, then, we will get on the move again. Barnes, you had better go in front with Davidson.' There ensued another interminable period (as it seemed to Basil) of stumbling and groping through the darkness, until the whisper, 'We are there at last,' was passed down the line.

'Now, Mitchell, have you got your torch ready?'

'In my hand, sir.'

'And your automatic in case you have to use it?'

'All ready, sir.'

'Then go ahead.'

Basil heard the click of the latch of the gate, and the dying sound of muffled footsteps, then in about thirty seconds a whisper:

'Time for us to start. Now follow me.'

With the Inspector in front, the men advanced in breathless silence. Basil trembled at the thought that he would see Doris within a few brief minutes, perhaps alive and well or perhaps—The imagination which made him a poet now evolved images of horror which tortured his heart like furies, and the inner conflict between exultant hope and wild despair seemed to tear his very soul in pieces.

And then the silence was broken by the violent barking of a dog, and the rasping of his chain against wood as he leaped wildly into the air in a desperate effort to get at the intruders.

Candlish broke into a run, reached the front door, and knocked loudly on it.

In a brief space of time the door opened on a chain, and a woman's voice asked:

'Who is there?'

'We are police officers, madam, and have a warrant to search this house. I must ask you to admit us without delay.'

The chain was removed and the door flung open.

Facing them they saw a woman of between fifty and sixty, gray haired, with thin inflexible lips, a strong chin and nose, and eyes which seemed to flash hatred and defiance at the intruders.

'Will you please show me your warrant?' she said.

Candlish held out that document for her inspection.

'You may come in, though you'll find nothing wrong in my house, and perhaps you will ask your friends at the back to make a little less noise,' said the woman with a sneer.

'Barnes,' said the Inspector, 'take this lady in there' (pointing to the door of a lighted room on the right), 'and keep her there till I come back. Mr James, will you be good enough to go through the kitchen and open the back door. Tell Davidson to stay there to see no one goes out, and bring the other two to me here.'

Candlish posted Pendleton to guard the front door, and then with the remaining three members of the party began a hasty search of the house, rushing with all speed from room to room, but except for the sour-faced old lady who had admitted them there was no sign of a human being.

Then began a second and more systematic search.

On the ground floor were two sitting rooms, one on either side of the entrance hall. The room on the left bore no signs of having been used for some time, but in that on the right in which the lady of the house had been left in charge of Detective Barnes, was a distinct smell of fresh tobacco smoke, and in an ash tray on the table were a number of cigarette ends, one of which still felt hot when Candlish examined it. On a chair was a copy of the current issue of the *Evening Times*.

The entrance to the kitchen was from the far end of the hall. It was a large room with all the marks of constant occupation. A fire was burning in the range, and the number of used plates and other debris suggested that a meal had recently been served to at least three or four persons.

On the upper floor was a long landing running from the front to the back of the house. Opening out of it to the left were a large bedroom in front and a bathroom behind, and to the right two bedrooms, a large one in front and a small one at the back. The room on the left did not appear to be in use, but in the front room on the right side the bed was made, and there were female garments in a hanging cupboard and in a chest of drawers.

'This is evidently where the old lady sleeps,' said Candlish, after a cursory examination. 'Now for the rooms at the back.'

The rooms at the back of the first floor were cut off from the rest of the house by a strong partition door, which divided the landing into two unequal portions. On the front of the door were two stout bolts, and in it was a sliding panel. Those windows in the shut-off portion, which looked out into the enclosed yard by the back door were barred, and two others in the side walls of the house were boarded up.

'This has been used as a prison,' said Mitchell, 'and the prisoner was here not many minutes ago, for this tea is still warm,' he added, as he picked up a teapot which, with a plate of roughly cut bread and butter and a cup and saucer, formed the equipment of a tray which stood on the dressing-table in the bedroom.

'Ah!' exclaimed Basil, as he stooped and picked up a bright object from the carpeted floor in front of the barred window,

'Miss Lyttleton has certainly been here, for this is her locket. My God, what have the brutes done with her?'

'I should not be surprised if Miss Lyttleton put that there for us to find,' said the Inspector. 'At any rate we know for certain that she was in this room alive not many minutes ago. Mr James, will you be good enough to relieve Barnes for a few minutes, and send him up to me?'

'Why certainly,' replied the American.

'Barnes,' said the Inspector a moment later, 'where does this lane lead to?'

'It is a blind alley, sir, made apparently to lead to this farm and for nothing else.'

'And behind the house, what is there?'

'A group of farm buildings, sheds, and barns, and beyond fields.'

'Then that is where our quarry must have gone, and we must lose no time in getting on their track again.'

By this time the party had descended the stairs.

'Pendleton,' said their leader, 'you must stay here and see that the old woman doesn't get up to any mischief. Mitchell, you take Davidson and Mr James and work round the yard to the left, looking into all the buildings. Mr Dawson and Barnes will accompany me to the right.'

'Hallo, what's this?' exclaimed the American, as he was crossing the threshold. 'I am sure I saw something bright as the Inspector's torch flashed on the ground by the door.' He stooped and picked up a small object which he held out to Basil.

'Do you recognise this?' he questioned.

'It is Miss Lyttleton's ring: I know it quite well,' was the agitated reply.

'Don't be alarmed, Mr Dawson, the young lady must have dropped it as a guide to us to show in which direction she has been taken. Something must have alarmed her jailers quite recently—damn that dog, what an infernal noise he is making—

and they, without having time to cover up all their traces, must have rushed upstairs and dragged her down and out of the back of the house. They cannot possibly have gone far in this darkness.'

The two search parties had only just begun their examination of the farm buildings when they were startled by the muffled sound of a shot followed by the tinkle of falling glass, and then in an interval of the barking they were aware of a voice calling, 'Help, help!'

'This way!' shouted Burton James, flashing his torch in the direction of a large stone-built erection in the middle of the yard.

The whole party rushed after him and threw themselves against the double doors, which, under the pressure of the weight and muscle of Barnes and Davidson, soon gave way.

They found themselves in a large compartment divided by partitions, which had once been the farm stables.

'Where are you? Is Miss Lyttleton there?' they shouted.

'In the loft above—there is a ladder in the small room. Be quick,' was the reply.

Basil rushed to the far end of the stables, followed by the others; there they found a partially closed door which they flung wide open.

Before them was a small room which had apparently in the past been used as a harness room. A ladder in one corner led upwards to a square opening in the ceiling.

Basil tore up the ladder, followed closely by Candlish and the rest of the party; and in a very few seconds they had all scrambled through the trap-door. The loft proved to be a long, low room, running the whole length of the harness room and stable. The trap door was at one end, and in the opposite wall, over the entrance to the stable, was a window. A sack had been hung over it to screen the light of a lantern which stood on the floor from the eyes of anyone entering the farm yard. By the side of the lantern was Doris Lyttleton, who held in her hand a large automatic pistol with which she covered the bodies of two men, who were standing against the opposite wall with their faces to it and their hands well above their heads. On the floor behind her was a second pistol, and in the air was the acrid smell of powder.

'Don't move an inch, either of you, or I shall fire,' she was saying as the rescue party entered the room.

'I can't see who you are,' she continued, without looking round, 'but these two men have been holding me as a prisoner for—'

She got no further, for almost simultaneously she was caught in Basil's hungry arms, while the Inspector and his assistants seized and handcuffed the two men.

'David Saunders and Frederick Saunders,' said Candlish gravely, 'I hold a warrant for your arrest on a charge of murder. And I warn you that anything you say may be used as evidence against you.'

CHAPTER XIX

'A woman, true, but what a woman!'
The Traitor's Wooing

Two days later a gathering took place in the Chief Inspector's room at Scotland Yard, at which the persons most interested in the solution of the Lyttleton case were present. Doris Lyttleton, dressed in black, her face pale and worn as the result of all that she had undergone, Basil Dawson, Burton James, Detective-Sergeant Mitchell and Candlish himself.

Said the latter after the first greetings were over and all were seated:

'The honours of the day belong to Miss Lyttleton, who, single-handed, captured both the criminals.'

'She would not have caught them at all, unless the police had raided the house, and even after catching them, she would not have been able to keep them,' replied Doris.

'The capture of the Saunders brothers was important enough,' said Basil; 'but the main thing after all was the finding of Miss Lyttleton.'

'Not so,' said Doris. 'The main thing was the discovery of poor father's fate, and the arrest of the treacherous scoundrels who killed him.'

'At any rate,' interposed Burton James, 'as all three things were achieved at one and the same time, it does not matter which part of the achievement was the most important.'

'I am going to make a suggestion,' said Candlish. 'We none of us know the full story of the last week's happenings, and if you are all as curious as I am, you will not be satisfied till you have heard it. I propose that Miss Lyttleton should begin by telling us all about her adventures, and then I will give you the story of how we solved the mystery of her abduction and her father's murder.'

'I am sure you will not misunderstand me and think me unfeeling,' said Doris, 'when I say that the news of my father's fate, dreadful as it was, came as a sort of relief after all the suspense and anxiety of the past months.'

'I experienced what that kind of suspense is like last week,' replied Basil. 'Hell itself could be no worse.'

'Yes,' remarked James, 'that is so, and nowadays no one doubts that all is well with the dead, and that, whether consciousness survives the great change or not, at any rate no harm can come to them.'

'Thank you, Mr James,' said Doris, 'that is just what I feel, but after all there is the personal loss for which no philosophy can console.

'I don't know exactly how much of what happened to me you were able to find out, Mr Candlish,' she began, 'so the best thing I can do, perhaps, is to tell you what occurred from the beginning. It was just a week ago this morning that I heard a loud knock at the door, and a moment later one of the maids came into the room where I was sitting, and said that a chauffeur had come in a motor-car with a letter for me, and that he was waiting in the hall for an answer.

'I opened the envelope which she handed me and found in it a letter from my father's cousin, Horace—at least it purported to be from him, but I suppose it must have been forged by that wretched man Saunders. The writer said that important news of my father had been received, and asked me to come at once in the car, when he would tell me all about it.

'I have often thought since that I was unwise and rash to take the letter at its face value without being struck by the improbabilities of its story; but I had been so anxious about my father, and was so excited at the thought of at last getting news of him, that I did not wait to think, or even ask the man where he was going to take me. I just sent Thomson back to tell him that I would accompany him. Then, after writing a hasty note to Mr Dawson, and rushing upstairs to put on my hat and coat, I got into the car. It was then for the first time that I thought of inquiring where I was being taken to.

'"To where Mr Horace Lyttleton is staying, madam," was the reply. "It is only about half an hour's run." I was still so excited that I did not trouble to question the man further, and when the car was stopped once or twice by the traffic I simply chafed for it to start again.

'Even when we got out on the country roads beyond London I just vaguely thought that we were probably making for Hillborough, where the Horace Lyttletons live; and I had no suspicion whatever that anything was wrong until the car swerved round suddenly into the little narrow lane which leads up to the house where I was imprisoned. However, the time was so short that before I could collect my thoughts the car had drawn up at the end of the lane, and the chauffeur was holding open a gate for me to enter. "Is Mr Lyttleton staying here?" I questioned.

'"Yes, madam, this is the house," he replied.

'The door was opened by the old woman you saw, who was, as I learned later, the mother of the two Saunders.'

('She is now safely lodged in Holloway Gaol,' interposed Candlish.)

'I said, "Is Mr Horace Lyttleton here?"

'"Yes, he is," she replied, "are you Miss Lyttleton?"

'When I had answered her, she said that she was to show me up to a room where I could take off my things; so I followed her upstairs into a room at the back of the house. I had thrown my hat and driving coat down on the bed, when my attention was attracted for a moment by the appearance of one of the windows, which had been boarded up. Before I realised what was happening, the old woman had snatched up my hat and coat and slipped out of the room, and the next thing I heard was the banging and bolting of a door.

'In a moment I realised that I had been tricked, and I rushed out of the room on to the landing, the back part of which I found to be shut off by a stout partition door. I shouted: "Please open the door at once," but there was no reply, and I could hear the woman's footsteps retreating along the landing and down the stairs. I then tried the other windows in the shut-off rooms and on the landing, but found that they were all barred, and that they looked out into a narrow enclosed courtyard at the back of the house.

'Of course I was frightened, but with my fear was mixed a grim sort of pleasure, because I felt that the people who had imprisoned me were most likely the same as those responsible for my father's disappearance, so I made up my mind to make the best of the situation, and, if I could, turn it to advantage.

'I shouted through the windows and banged the door in turns, but no one appeared, and as time wore on I began to fear that my captors were going to let me starve. However, about four o'clock in the afternoon I heard the woman's voice at the partition door. She said:

'"If you will give me a solemn promise not to try to get past me, I will give you some tea."

'I was so hungry and exhausted that I promised, and the bolts were withdrawn, the door opened, and a tray of tea pushed through.

'"I want you to understand this," said the woman, as she stood in the doorway, "if you behave yourself and keep quiet, you'll be well treated, but if you try any nonsense, you'll get no food. This house is a long way from any other, and you will have no chance of being heard, however much you scream, so you had better make up your mind to be reasonable."

'I then told her that she had no right whatever to keep me there, and insisted on being allowed to go free, but at this she laughed in a horrid way and went out, locking and bolting the door behind her.

'About seven o'clock the woman brought me some more food, which she passed in through a sliding panel in the partition door, saying as she handed me the tray, "You had better be quick with your meal, as you will be wanted downstairs in half an hour's time."

'True to her word, at half-past seven she returned, and invited me to follow her downstairs. I hesitated at first whether I should refuse, but it seemed that by going I might at least gather some information about my captors, while by refusing to move I might provoke them to use actual violence; so I went, and was taken downstairs into a sitting-room which opened out of the entrance hall.

'Two men rose to greet me as I entered, and to my amazement and stupefaction I recognised one of them as Mr David Saunders, my father's manager. Thinking at first that he must have heard of my abduction and come to rescue me, I felt I can't tell you how much relieved, and I went forward to greet him with hand outstretched.

'"Oh, Mr Saunders," I said, "I am so pleased to see you. I have been inveigled here by a lying story and have been locked up in a room for hours."

'"Miss Lyttleton," was his reply, "please sit down for a moment, as I have something important to say to you; but first of all I would like to introduce you to my brother Frederick, who is also in the employ of Lyttletons."

'When Frederick spoke, his voice seemed familiar, and I learned later on that he had played the part of the chauffeur who had pretended to be the messenger of Horace Lyttleton.

'"What is it you wish to say to me, Mr Saunders?" I asked, when we were seated, and the younger brother had left the room.

'"I am a plain, blunt business man, Miss Lyttleton," he replied, "so I will come at once to the point."

'"I am waiting for it," said I.

'"The point is that I love you, and wish you to become my wife."

'I sprang to my feet. "Mr Saunders," I said, "let me repeat my request that you let me out of this horrible house. As you know that I am engaged to another man, your proposal is an insult, and I cannot listen to another word."

'He remained seated and replied coolly, "You will never leave this house, except as my wife, so you had better see reason at once."

'There was a sort of cold determination about the way he spoke that made me shudder, but I pretended not to care, and snapped my fingers in front of his face.

'"Then you are responsible for my abduction," I said. "I thought you were an honest man, but I find that my father has trusted a scoundrel all these years. As for me, I regard your threats and your proposal of marriage with the same contempt."

'"You'll know better before you are much older," was his reply.

'"Here Mother, Fred," he called, "Miss Lyttleton is in an unreasonable mood, will you see her safely back to her room?"'

'The next four days were very like the first; and each evening I was brought downstairs to listen to the pleadings and threats of the elder Saunders. On Saturday, however, the brothers evidently arrived at the house much earlier than usual, for it was about half-past four in the afternoon when the woman came to fetch me.

'I could see at a glance when I entered the sitting-room that something had happened which had upset the peace of mind of David and Frederick. The manner of both was hurried and anxious, and when I was left alone with David he wasted no time in persuasion, but began at once in his hypocritical way to threaten me.

"'I am in great difficulty, Miss Lyttleton," said he, "and I am sure you will appreciate it. The fact is the police are making quite a lot of impertinent inquiries into my affairs, and I have reason to think that they actually suspect me of being concerned in your disappearance. Absurd, is it not? Well, they will no doubt discover in time that this house was left to me by my late uncle, a very worthy farmer he was, in which case they may come here to look for you. Can't you see what an awkward position I am in?"

"'In other words," I said, "you are on the eve of being found out for the villain you are."

"'My dear Miss Lyttleton, or may I say Miss Doris," he replied in his sleek, oily way, "you quite misunderstand the position. I have not the slightest intention of being found out. No, your continued existence, except as Mrs David Saunders, would be so dangerous to me, that unless you agree to my suggestion, I shall be forced—most reluctantly, no doubt—but forced—to bring your earthly career to a premature end. I would call your attention to the usefulness of a nice large garden such as we have here, as a private burial ground."

'I was thoroughly frightened by this time, but I managed to screw up courage to laugh as I replied—

"'You must have been reading too many sensational novels lately, Mr Saunders."

'He merely said in a grim way:

"'Laugh if you please, but by this time tomorrow you will be either Mrs Saunders or nothing."

"'How could you prevent me from appealing to the clergyman even if I did pretend to consent?" I asked, anxious now to gain time.

"'I had thought of that," he replied, "I should expect you to write a letter at once to Mr Basil Dawson, saying that as you were going to marry me, you had thought it no harm to anticipate the ceremony by a few days, so we had been staying in the country as man and wife. If you wrote such a letter, you would not want to avoid the marriage."

(Doris shuddered as she forced herself to go on.)

'I then said,' she continued, 'that he could not expect me to surrender without further time for consideration.

'"You can go back to your room, and at ten o'clock tomorrow morning I shall expect your final decision," was his answer.

'I went upstairs and flung myself down on my bed in sheer despair. Of course, I had made my choice as soon as the alternatives had been stated; but, though I was determined to die, I do not pretend that I liked the prospect. To be murdered and then hidden away—and yet that is what happened to my poor dear father.'

'You must remember, dear,' said Basil, 'that your father did not suffer at all: he was killed suddenly. And it is the anticipation of death which is so terrible, not the mere act of dying.'

'Thank you for reminding me of it, Basil,' said Doris, as she continued. 'I must have lain on my bed for quite a long time, when I heard a commotion downstairs, and very soon my door was opened and I was told roughly to come down. Mrs Saunders began hurriedly to smooth the bed and to tidy up the room, and I heard her say to her son Frederick that she would have every trace of my presence hidden in the event of the police coming, as they thought possible.

'Under the pretext of arranging my hair, I stopped for a moment before the dressing table, took off my locket, and while the woman's back was turned, flung it down on the floor in front of the window, praying inwardly that my enemies might not see it, and my friends not overlook it.

'I was then hustled downstairs into the sitting-room, but as I went I loosened one of my rings with the intention of dropping it just outside whichever door I was taken through.

'David Saunders tied my hands together behind my back with a table napkin, and another he fastened round my mouth.

'Then the two brothers pushed me out through the back door, where I dropped the ring, stumbling so as to smother the noise. They each carried a pistol, and Frederick went in front with a lantern. I heard the old lady bolting the back door behind us as we went through the yard. All this time I was wriggling my hands about, and I could feel that the knot of the napkin was getting looser. We crossed the farmyard into the old stable, the door of which David locked behind us.

'"If it is the police," said he to his brother, "they will find nothing in the house, and when they go away, we can take our fair guest back there. I promised her till tomorrow morning to make up her mind, and I have always been a man of my word."

'When we came to the ladder, Frederick went up first to push the trap-door aside, and when he had done it he came down again and the two of them hauled me up into the loft, where they pushed me on to a heap of sacks in the corner of the end nearest the trap-door and farthest from the window.

'"We must put out the lantern," said Frederick, "or the light will be visible from the back of the house."

'"Better still," said his brother, "cover up the window with a sack, then we can keep our light and be quite invisible at the same time; but first let us pull up the ladder and replace the trap."

'"No, the window is the most important; we must get that covered up first. Here, lend a hand," said Frederick, taking up a sack and putting his pistol down on the floor by the lantern.

'David also dropped his weapon and joined his brother at the window.

'It's now or never, thought I—my hands were already loose, and it did not take a second to untie the gag. I then crept across the floor towards the pistols, which were only a few feet away from where I was supposed to be lying helpless.

'My heart was in my mouth lest either of the two brothers should turn round; but they continued absorbed in their task of ripping open the sack and stretching it across some old nails which they found conveniently placed in the window frame.

'In a space of time which must have been very short, though it seemed ages, I had reached the pistols, and taking up one of them, I pushed the other behind me.

'My jailers must have been very astonished—they certainly looked it—when they heard my invitation to hold their hands above their heads.

'"Take care," I said, "I know how to aim a pistol"—which was quite true, for dad and I used to amuse ourselves sometimes by shooting at a mark in the garden—"and I shall not hesitate to shoot if either of you attempt to play any tricks."

'I then made them turn round to face the wall—one on each side of the window. But what was I to do next? If I left my post for a moment to escape down the ladder, they would catch me before I got half-way down. I shouted "Help, help," but I felt that the sound would never carry through the glass and sacking to the ears of a rescue party who might be in the house. It seemed that I could do nothing but wait on the chance that the police would come into the stable. In the meantime I knew that something was going on, as I could hear the noise the dog was making.

'And then a thought struck me. I would break the window. No sooner said than done. I aimed the pistol at the middle of the sack and fired. The noise in that low room was stunning, but I had the presence of mind to say, "Keep still, you two cowards, or I shall shoot you." I then raised my voice again and called for help as loudly as I could. What was my delight to hear your answering shouts, which proved that at last you had heard and were coming to the rescue.

'The rest you know.'

The Chief Inspector rose from his chair, bowed to Doris, and said solemnly:

'Miss Lyttleton, you are a very brave and very resourceful woman.'

CHAPTER XX

'With opportunity for steed and necessity for spur, he rode gaily to the devil.'

Collection of 16th Century Novelists

'Now, then, Inspector, it is for you to carry out your share of the bargain,' said Burton James, as he lit another cigarette. 'I feel at present as if my mind were full of the bits of a jig-saw puzzle which I could not make into a coherent picture.'

'None of you,' began Candlish, 'would have leisure or patience to listen to a repetition of all the detailed history of the case, nor indeed have I the time to narrate it. You all know part of the story, and I think the best thing I can do is to go rapidly over the ground from the beginning, embodying what the police have found out, and what David Saunders has told us in a statement he made yesterday. Those parts of the story which are already well known to all of you, I shall refer to in the briefest possible manner.

'David Saunders,' began the Chief Inspector, 'is a very clever man, and like many other clever men, he is both ambitious and unscrupulous. The latter characteristic, however, lay latent for many years. As long as all goes well with a man of that type, he will be honest and exact in his dealings; but let him get into difficulties, and then he will stick at nothing to extricate himself.

'Saunders, under his cautious and phlegmatic exterior, concealed the soul of a gambler. Up to a point he was an unusually successful one. Do not think, I pray you, that I hold Puritanical views as to the wickedness of gambling. It naturally has an irresistible attraction for men who have ambition, but lack money (and all that money implies) to push them up the

189

ladder of success. To such a man gambling appears to offer the only possible escape from drudgery and poverty; the only possible path to promotion from the ranks of the industrial army.

'No, my objection to gambling is not that it is wicked, but that it is foolish. Whether on the turf, the green table, or the stock exchange, the amateur is always up against professional players, and the dice are always loaded against him.

'Saunders and his brother were both unmarried. Their mother, from whom they have appeared to have inherited the more brilliant as well as the undesirable sides of their characters, kept house for them. Their incomes were fair ones—good, indeed, for men who had only their own ability to sell. But mediocrity had no charms for either of them, and they aspired to become themselves founders of a great financial house in the city.

'Their most amiable trait—and we must be just to scoundrels—was the strong affection which existed between them and their mother, which, when they definitely turned to evil courses, made the three of them so powerful and so dangerous a combination.

'For years Saunders had dabbled in speculation; in which the inside knowledge he gained through his position at Lyttletons was of the greatest assistance. His operations, though comparatively small, were in the main successful, and by the early part of this year he had accumulated a working capital of about eight thousand pounds.

'But in the meantime the tastes of the brothers were expanding. Frederick was anxious to marry and set up a household of his own, but the salary of three hundred and fifty pounds a year, which he drew from the office, appeared quite inadequate for the establishment he had in view. Moreover, David had recently launched out into expenditure of various kinds, including the purchase of an electric motor-car (of which more anon), and generally they both felt that the time had come for a heroic attempt to storm the citadel of wealth.

'It was in April or May last that their opportunity seemed to come. Confidential information reached Lyttletons from their agents in Tientsin that the Russian "Whites" under Semenoff had won a great battle against the "Reds," and that almost certainly the whole of Siberia would speedily be restored to the régime of the Romanoffs, in which case, of course, the mining resources of the country would be handed over to the foreign financiers who had controlled them before the Revolution. Mr James Lyttleton apparently considered the news unreliable. At any rate he did not act on it, nor would he consent to any purchases of Siberian shares by the firm, but his cousin bought very heavily in his private capacity, and so did David Saunders. I may say that, while Saunders knew what Horace was doing, none of the partners were aware of the speculations of their implicitly trusted manager.

'Both Horace and Saunders bought on the cover system, that is, paying a deposit only on the shares, anticipating an immediate and heavy rise in their price, as soon as the news of Semenoff's success should be published. But like so many other great victories, it had taken place only in the imaginations of interested parties, and the Siberian shares, instead of going up, continued slowly but steadily to fall. At each settling day the two speculators were called upon, either to find more cover in the shape of large sums of ready money, or to sell out and lose all their capital. Horace managed to hang on somehow by mortgaging all his resources, and eventually only a few days ago another rumoured "White" victory created a temporary boom, during which he was able to sell out his holdings and to realise a considerable profit on his outlay.

'But Saunders had no resources to mortgage once his small capital was swallowed up. He accordingly, as he put it, "borrowed" money from the firm, and every settling day his defalcations were increased by some thousands of pounds. By the end of June his position was literally desperate, and as he could take no more of Lyttletons' money without imminent risk of discovery, he was compelled to let his holdings go.

'Imagine his position, then—all the savings of years lost and something like twenty thousand pounds besides. An amount which must certainly be missed by the firm in the near future, when the shortage would infallibly be traced to him. But retribution was nearer even than he thought, for on the morning of the thirtieth of June he was sent for by Mr James Lyttleton, who remarked that the firm's balances at the Bank of England and Glyn's were unusually low, and that he was going to get the auditors to prepare an *ad interim* statement of accounts.

'Saunders knew that if the auditors came in it would only be a question of hours before he was under arrest for defrauding the firm, and he did not intend to be arrested if he could help it.

'That evening he and his brother held a prolonged consultation, the result of which was that they decided deliberately and in cold blood to kill Mr James Lyttleton, and by implicating his cousin Horace in the murder, to get rid of him also from the business; in which case they reckoned that the owners of Lyttletons being Mr Menzies, whom they regarded as a fool, Myles Lyttleton, whom they looked on as an idler, and a woman, Miss Doris Lyttleton, the real control would fall into the hands of David, who would then be in a position to cover up his speculations, until by successful stock exchange operations the money could be replaced. He would also be able to secure the promotion of Frederick, and the two brothers saw themselves with the eye of imagination taken eventually into the firm as managing partners.

'Horace and his son were, they knew, out of the country and their house empty. How better promote their designs then than by inveigling James Lyttleton to Holly Lodge and killing him there? Accordingly as a first step David, who was an accomplished penman, wrote a letter to James in Horace's script and with Horace's signature, saying that he had returned home hurriedly from France as he had received some very important information with regard to the business of the firm; that, as he was unwell, he would be unable to come to the city for a few days, and asking his cousin to attend at the office before the staff arrived on the following morning, so that he could speak to him on the telephone without the possibility of interruption. Frederick then motored over to Hillborough, and posted the letter there in time for the night post. He took with him a supply of food and also his motor cycle strapped to the roof of the car. From the post office he drove to Holly Lodge, the grounds of which he entered unnoticed by anyone (you will remember that the car was electrically propelled and therefore almost silent in its action). He was a fair amateur mechanic, and he found no difficulty in opening the doors both of the motor shed and of the house itself, where he awaited the arrival of his victim. I should mention that he had the day before begun his holidays, so that his absence from the office would be fully accounted for.

'In the morning David Saunders rang up from a public call office; and, imitating as well as he could the tones of Horace Lyttleton, asked to be put through to the senior partner. He said, speaking as Horace, that he had received a letter from one of the cashiers confessing to having defrauded the firm of a considerable sum of money, and he asked his partner to visit him at Hillborough that afternoon without fail to discuss the matter and to come to a decision upon it. It was then that Mr James, evidently seriously perturbed, gave expression to those phrases which were overheard by the office boy: "decision, clear out all together, prosecution."

'Mr Lyttleton is said to have looked worried during the rest of the day, and at half-past three he left the office and drove in a taxi to Victoria, where he caught the 4.10 train to Hillborough.

'As soon as he was out of the office, David sent for the second office boy, Davis, and gave him a telegram which he said Mr Lyttleton wanted to have despatched from Euston Station. The boy forgot it and went to a cinema, which accounts for its not having been despatched till 5.30 p.m.

'In the meantime Mr Lyttleton arrived at Hillborough and walked to his cousin's house. All unsuspecting he knocked at the door, which was opened by Frederick, who, as he entered, swung the door to behind him, and at the same time struck him violently on the head with a heavy spanner which he had found in the motor shed. Poor Mr Lyttleton must have died instantaneously. The murderer appears to have been absolutely callous. He transferred the money and the papers (including one thousand pounds in bank notes) from his victim's pocket to his own, then dragged the body into a cupboard, and washed up the small quantity of blood which had fallen in the hall. Finally he prepared himself a meal, and sat down to wait for his brother, who was due to arrive after dark.

'It was then that he was startled by a newspaper being pushed into the letter box on the front door. It was the current number of the *Hillborough Times*. In idle curiosity he began to read it, and came across an account of the death two days before of a gentleman from New Zealand, who had been staying at the County Hotel, whose body, it was stated, had been taken to the mortuary to await burial on the following day.

'He knew that the mortuary was situated in grounds which were divided by a wall from the garden of Holly Lodge, and he was struck by the possibilities of the situation. By the time David arrived, which was about a quarter to ten, he had a scheme cut and dried. It was so ingenious that David readily fell in with it.

'After waiting until midnight so as to be sure that every one was in bed, they carried Mr Lyttleton's body through the garden and somehow managed to get it over the wall, from which it was only about fifty yards to the door of the mortuary. The lock presented no difficulty to Frederick, and it was a simple matter to unscrew the coffin they found in the chapel, to remove the corpse which was in it, and to substitute that of Mr Lyttleton. They took the grave clothes off the stranger's body and stuffed them back into the coffin. When they had screwed the lid on again, they made their first serious mistake. A wreath had been placed on the coffin, and this they put back in a different position to that which it had originally occupied. The disturbance made by the mortuary keeper's wife, when she found in the morning that the wreath had been moved, was one of the things that eventually directed our attention to the mortuary, and in that way contributed materially to the discovery of the crime.

'Having, as they thought, removed all signs of their visit to the mortuary, they conveyed the stranger's body to Holly Lodge, and vested it in clothes which they took from Mr Myles Lyttleton's bedroom, after first cutting off all marks by which they might be identified. They, however, left the imprint on the collar by which we were able to trace it to a Hillborough tradesman.

'Their next step was to clear up all traces of their presence in the house, which they did very successfully. The only clue they left behind them was a copy of the *Daily Telegraph* for the first of July. They then got out the motor, placed the body in it, and after making sure that no one was about in the street outside, drove out of the entrance gate.

'Once beyond the town the motor cycle was taken down from the car, and Frederick rode off at full speed to catch the 2.30 train from St Pancras to Liverpool. He did not risk leaving the cycle in the cloak-room, where at that time of night he would be a noticeable visitor, but dismounting in one of the slummy streets on the south of the Euston Road, left the machine standing against the wall in a narrow alley, after first removing the number plate. His surmise that the finder of the cycle would quietly annex it, proved correct, for its discovery was never reported to Scotland Yard.'

CHAPTER XXI

'Zindomar, that mighty king,
Set his heart on conquering
All the world to write his name
Large upon the scroll of fame.
But he stumbled on a hole,
Burrowed by a purblind mole,
Fell and broke his neck, which brought
All his soaring schemes to nought.'

Contes Persanes: trans. BILLINGHURST

'ON his arrival at the great Lancashire port, Frederick had some breakfast at the Central Station, then crossed over to Lime Street where he despatched the telegram to Miss Lyttleton in her father's name. He then booked his passage to New York by the *Ruritania*, and purchased a trunk and the clothes and other things necessary for his journey. With these he drove to the Lime Street Hotel, engaged a room, in which he slept until one o'clock, when he had lunch, paid his bill, and drove down to the landing stage, from which his steamer was due to sail at three-thirty that afternoon.

'His doings in New York are already known to you. It was a blunder on his part to enter into conversation with the clerk at the hotel and so to attract attention to his movements. The collar that he left behind him was one that he had taken from Myles Lyttleton's room, when he was waiting at Holly Lodge for the arrival of his victim. It was left intentionally so as to serve as an additional link in the chain of evidence connecting Horace and his son with the murder. The spectacles, which he had taken from Mr Lyttleton's pocket, were used and left in the cab in order to puzzle the police when the inevitable inquiries were made.

197

'You will notice that there was a certain inconsistency in the various actions of the conspirators. Their original scheme of immediately implicating Horace and Myles had been modified; and their perfected plan provided, as it were, two lines of defence: firstly, they hoped that the exchange of bodies in the mortuary would make the murder absolutely safe from discovery; and secondly, if detection were imminent at any future time, they thought that they would be able by the use of such a device as the letter which David subsequently forged in Horace's name, to direct the attention of the police away from themselves.

'While Frederick was on his way to Liverpool, David drove the car along the Surrey roads into Southshire; and there in an unfrequented part of the downs (which he knew well) he turned the car off the road and ran it over the intervening grassland to the banks of a small stream, into which he threw the New Zealander's body.

'He forgot that the imprint of his tyres would be left on the road where the car swerved off on to the grass; and the fact that those imprints correspond with the tyres of his car, which is now in our hands, will be an important item in the evidence for the Crown at the trial.

'David Saunders was in his place at the office on the morning of the second of July, and his brother returned from America before the last day of his holiday. About that time the principal outdoor clerk developed an illness, and David arranged that Frederick should take over his work in order that he might have more freedom of movement should any unexpected crisis arise which might call for sudden action.

'July wore on; Mr Dawson went to New York; and on his return the police were called in to help discover what had happened to Mr Lyttleton.'

'Excuse me,' interposed Basil at this point, 'you referred to the one thousand pounds which Mr Lyttleton drew out of the bank on that last morning. Have you any theory as to why he should have wanted so large a sum?'

'No, I must admit,' was the reply, 'that I do not know why he required the money. None of the evidence we have collected affords any clue to it. But Mr Lyttleton was a very rich man, and it is quite possible that he did not regard one thousand pounds as an unusually large amount to carry in his pocket-book.'

'My father sometimes did carry large sums about with him,' said Doris. 'I have often remonstrated with him and urged him to be careful. He was very fond of buying pictures, and he paid regular visits to some of the dealers' galleries in the West End, when it was his custom to pay in notes for anything he fancied and to bring it straight home with him in a cab.'

'I am afraid we shall never know exactly,' said Candlish, as he resumed his narrative.

'From the first the plans of the Saunders brothers began to go awry. Instead of leaving the control of the business to David as he had anticipated, both Mr Menzies and Mr Horace Lyttleton attended at the office regularly; and it was apparent that the discovery of the faked accounts was inevitable, at the very latest when the accountants came in for the usual interim audit at the end of the Michaelmas quarter.

'Matters were, however, brought to a head when David went on important office business to see Horace Lyttleton at Hillborough on the August bank holiday. As he walked up to Holly Lodge from the station, he passed the mortuary gate just as I was standing there talking to Whiteley, the mortuary keeper. He seems then to have had a fit of nerves, and forgetting for the moment that, even if the exchange of the bodies was discovered, suspicion would fall not on himself but on Horace and Myles Lyttleton, he decided to silence me before I had time to communicate with the Yard. He therefore hung about the town after leaving Holly Lodge, keeping an eye on my movements and waiting for an opportunity to attack me. You know what followed—how I was left for dead and my papers stolen; but here again the would-be murderer bungled his work, or I should not be alive today to tell you this story.

'Frederick, when he heard what had happened, was furious, and upbraided his brother bitterly for what he had done. His contention was that up to that point there had been suspicion but no evidence that any crime had been committed at all, while now it was almost certain that I should be reported missing, and that my body would be found and would give the police something definite to go on. The whole elaborate scheme was, in fact, endangered. He therefore insisted that steps should be taken immediately to set the police definitely on the track of Horace and his son in connection with Mr Lyttleton's disappearance, and so by implication to bring them under suspicion of having murdered me. (You will remember that until last Friday both David and Frederick thought I was dead.)

'So it was that David set to work to concoct the letter purporting to have been written by Horace on the twenty-ninth of June: a letter which he first of all placed between the sheets of blotting paper on Mr Lyttleton's desk, then arranged to have found by an office boy whom he instructed to turn over every scrap of paper in the room in search of another document, which was all the time safely in his own possession. The forged letter was, as you know, handed to Sergeant Mitchell when he opportunely called at Winchester House the day after I was put *hors de combat*.

'It was on this occasion that David Saunders made another mistake in his attempt to strengthen suspicion against Horace Lyttleton. He tried to make the office boy tell Mitchell that he had heard Mr James Lyttleton use the word "dissolution" during his eventful conversation on the telephone on the first of July, thus suggesting that he was quarrelling with and threatening a partner. The boy, however, was quite positive that he had not heard the word used at all, and the incident stuck in Mitchell's memory as a point against David's veracity.

'Frederick Saunders appears to have shown himself

throughout a harder, bolder, more adventurous scoundrel than his brother, and while he still loyally looked up to David as the head of the clan, it was he himself who was the leading spirit in the events which followed the attack on me.

'When on the evening of the same day David described to him the interview that he had with Mitchell, he roundly declared that the situation was desperate, and that something must be done at once to make their position secure. "I can see only one way in which this can be done," he said, "and that is for one or the other of us to marry Miss Lyttleton, whose husband will at once step into the position of senior partner of Lyttletons, and as such be in a position to put the accounts in order by making good the deficiency. If the attention of the police is not attracted to us by the discovery of this, we shall be safe enough in other directions; but if they once get on our track as having robbed the firm, then the whole story is bound to come out."

'He next proceeded to propose the abduction of Miss Lyttleton, who might, he felt sure, be forced under threats to agree to a marriage.

'David assented, and the brothers then decided to admit their mother to their confidence—it is only fair to the old lady to say that I believe she knew nothing about her sons' experiments in murder—and between the three of them a scheme was formulated.

'It sometimes occurs that careless people, when they have written a letter, fold up a blank sheet at the same time as that on which they have written. Now some months ago a Mr Vandeleur of The Gables, Wimbledon Common, had occasion to write to Lyttletons about some securities he was purchasing, and with his letter was a blank sheet of embossed notepaper, which David Saunders threw aside into a drawer when he opened the envelope.

'Remembering this, he decided to make use of it to baffle the police in connection with the contemplated abduction. So on the morning of the tenth, which was a Sunday, he went specially up to town to fetch it, and at the same time the original letter from Mr Vandeleur, whose handwriting he wished to imitate.

'David's skill as a forger was indubitable, and in other circumstances he might have won name and fame in the criminal underworld by the practice of that precarious profession.

'A letter was written in Mr Vandeleur's name and handwriting to the proprietor of a garage at Streatham, and on the following morning Frederick, who was supposed to have gone to Birmingham on the firm's business, bought a chauffeur's cap at Croydon, took the letter to Streatham, obtained the car on hire (as Mr Vandeleur's supposed employé, of course), and then drove off to Hampstead to deliver still another forged letter, which you have heard Miss Lyttleton describe.

'In making their plans the brothers had decided that their Purley house was quite unsuitable for the purpose of a prison and hiding place for Miss Lyttleton, but fortunately for their designs, Mrs Saunders was the owner of a house in an out-of-the-way position between Cheam and Ewell. It had been left to her by her brother, who had farmed the adjacent land; but this had since old John Saunders's death been bought by speculators with a view to eventual development as a building estate, and the house had from time to time been let furnished to London families, who preferred quiet and seclusion to the bustle and crush of a seaside resort.

'On the Sunday afternoon Frederick drove his mother to Haydock's Farm, which was the name of the house I have just referred to, with a supply of clothes and other necessaries.

'You have heard Miss Lyttleton's story of how she was deceived by the forged letter into accompanying her cousin's supposed chauffeur, and how she fared subsequently; how she was taken to Haydock's Farm, and how Mrs Saunders removed her hat and tussore driving coat, and locked her up in the shut-off portion of the upper floor of the house. What happened next was that the old woman put on the hat and coat and got into the car, which was driven by Frederick to Wimbledon. The motor was stopped deliberately just in front of a constable, and Frederick made some remark to him in order, no doubt, to call his attention to the car and its occupants. He then in full view of the constable drove on up to the front door of Mr Vandeleur's residence, The Gables, knocked, and when the door was opened, pretended to have mistaken the house, then, after some delay for the purpose of allowing the policeman to get out of hearing, he drove back again in the direction of Wimbledon; then to Haydock's Farm, where he left his mother, and eventually he returned the car to Young's garage at Streatham.

'On both occasions when the car was under observation, first by the constable and secondly by Mr Vandeleur's butler, its female occupant kept her face studiously turned away, while Miss Lyttleton's hat and coat were in full view.

'In this way a very plainly marked trail was laid right up to The Gables. Unfortunately, however, for the brothers, Mr Vandeleur's personality, character, and position were such that it was impossible for a single moment to suspect him of being concerned in Miss Lyttleton's abduction. If David had been in a position to make use of the notepaper of almost anyone else, the ruse might have been successful in at any rate delaying the solution of the mystery.

'As you know, a reward of one thousand pounds was offered for news of Miss Lyttleton. This offer brought to the Yard a mass of irrelevant correspondence, but with it came a letter from a Sutton resident who had observed the car containing Miss Lyttleton and Frederick as it halted in Cheam. The area of our search was materially reduced by this, and I think that the writer of the letter has fairly earned at least a portion of the thousand pounds.'

'He shall have it all,' said Doris.

'The final crisis was precipitated,' continued Candlish, 'when Mitchell and I interviewed and questioned each member of the

staff at Winchester House on Friday evening. We hoped that
my sudden and unexpected appearance would shock the guilty
man, if, as appeared probable, he was a member of the staff,
into betraying himself; but unfortunately Frederick Saunders
had been sent that morning on some business to the office of
the Paymaster-General in Whitehall and had recognised me as
I was on my way back to the Yard from lunch. He had the
shock of his life, but unluckily I did not see him, and he was
able to warn his brother by telephone.

'Both of them were accordingly prepared for my visit, but
both in the cross-examination I gave them made damaging
admissions. Moreover, they gave contradictory accounts of the
circumstances under which they were familiar with the Cheam
district. It is true, certainly, that another clerk also fell under
suspicion, but subsequent inquiries cleared him.

'Two results followed our interview with the brothers. We
suspected them, and they in turn realised that we did so. Both
parties accordingly decided to lose no time. Detective officers
were sent to Purley and Cheam to pursue inquiries, and by six
o'clock on Saturday evening reports had reached me which left
no doubt that the two Saunders were responsible for Miss
Lyttleton's abduction, and that she was imprisoned at Haydock's
Farm.'

'Should I be indiscreet, Inspector, if I were to ask what those
reports were?' interrupted Burton James. 'This is one of the
queerest stories I have ever come across, and I don't want to
miss any details.'

'I will tell you with pleasure,' was the reply. 'Mitchell here
went straight down to Purley on Saturday morning. He was
lucky enough to be able to get one of the maids at 3 Haselden
Road, where the Saunders family resided, to talk—(very fascin-
ating chap is Mitchell! Don't blush, my boy)—and from her he
ascertained firstly, that Frederick Saunders had been away from
home for about a fortnight at the beginning of July (although
he had told me that he had spent his summer holidays quietly

at home); and secondly, that Mrs Saunders had left Purley on the previous Sunday in the car with her younger son, who had returned home a few hours later without her, and that she had, been away ever since. He was also able to get a peep at the car, when he noted that the tyres corresponded exactly with the tracks left on the surface of the road in Southshire at the place where the New Zealander's body was found.

'With this information he returned to town, and came straight along to my flat in Upper Gloucester Place. While he was there, the men I had sent to Cheam telephoned the result of their inquiries, stating that Haydock's Farm, which Frederick Saunders had said that he used to know when his uncle was alive, was, according to the evidence of the local council's rate book, occupied by a Mrs Henry Saunders, that someone was in residence at the house, and that two men answering to the description of David and Frederick, had arrived there about four o'clock, walking from the direction of Cheam, and they had not yet been seen to leave.

'This was enough for me, and I decided on immediate action.

'Mitchell and I set off at once for Scotland Yard and completed our preparations. The opportune arrival of Mr James offered a ready way of communicating with Mr Dawson, and the expedition set off with the results you all know.

'To complete the story, however, I should add that the Saunders brothers after Friday's interview felt sure that we should sooner or later raid Haydock's Farm, but they did not expect us to get there as soon as we did, and they anticipated having Saturday and Sunday to clear up their business unmolested by the police.

'They had fully determined that, if Miss Lyttleton did not agree to marry David, she should be given the alternative of becoming Frederick's wife, and that, if she still proved obdurate, they would kill her, bury the body, and conceal every trace of her stay at the farm.

'But the gamblers had already had their last throw against

fate when they abducted Miss Lyttleton, and now they had lost
the game once and for all.

'You remember from Miss Lyttleton's story how they were
suddenly alarmed and tried to hide her and themselves in the
stable loft. It appears that they heard our car stop at the end
of the lane, and when after a couple of minutes it did not start
again, they scented danger. Even then they believed that,
failing to find them in the house, we should go away and leave
them to carry their villainous schemes through to completion.
Thanks, however, to Miss Lyttleton's pluck and quick-witted
resourcefulness, their plans were thwarted and they will now
have to suffer the penalties they so richly deserve.'

CHAPTER XXII

'The lights are out; the taverns close;
Both drunk and sober seek repose.'
                                    Ballad

THUS was the famous Lyttleton mystery finally solved.

It only remains to say that, when at Candlish's suggestion a special investigation of the accounts of the firm of Lyttleton, Menzies and Lyttleton was made by a famous firm of chartered accountants, an enormous deficit was revealed exceeding by many thousands of pounds the sum mentioned by David Saunders in his statement to the police.

Despite his inward chagrin at these heavy losses, Horace Lyttleton contrives to look more prosperous and more moneyed than ever, for, as he himself says, 'it does not pay to look as if you had lost money.'

Myles has married a smart barmaid, and those who knew them both say that she has made a *mésalliance.*

Andrew Young did not get the one thousand pounds reward, even though he threatened to bring actions against the police and Doris for withholding it. The solicitor whom he consulted, however, told him that he had no chance of succeeding, so he is now trying to make up for what he considers unjustly lost, by selling second-rate cars at first-rate prices to the wealthy social aspirants of Streatham.

Constable Higginson was given a stripe, but, despite it, his station superintendent considers him a hopeless fool. He still worships at the shrine of the great Sherlock Holmes, and dreams of impossible achievements.

Candlish and his wife continue to live in Upper Gloucester Place, happy because they have nothing to quarrel about.

As to Basil and Doris: they were married after the lapse of the usual year of mourning.

Like every other couple who make the great adventure, they are convinced that they will 'live happily ever after.' It is true that the general experience of mankind would appear to contradict their hopes; but what pair of lovers has ever heeded the general experience of mankind, or in the long run failed to contribute to it?

THE END

THE DETECTIVE STORY CLUB

FOR DETECTIVE CONNOISSEURS

recommends

"The Man with the Gun."

THE BLACKMAILERS

By THE MASTER OF THE FRENCH CRIME STORY—EMILE GABORIAU

EMILE GABORIAU is France's greatest detective writer. *The Blackmailers* is one of his most thrilling novels, and is full of exciting surprises. The story opens with a sensational bank robbery in Paris, suspicion falling immediately upon Prosper Bertomy, the young cashier whose extravagant living has been the subject of talk among his friends. Further investigation, however, reveals a network of blackmail and villainy which seems as if it would inevitably close round Prosper and the beautiful Madeleine, who is deeply in love with him. Can he prove his innocence in the face of such damning evidence?

THE REAL THING *from* SCOTLAND YARD!

THE CRIME CLUB

By FRANK FRÖEST, Ex-Supt. C.I.D., Scotland Yard, and George Dilnot

YOU will seek in vain in any book of reference for the name of The Crime Club. Its watchword is secrecy. Its members wear the mask of mystery, but they form the most powerful organisation against master criminals ever known. The Crime Club is an international club composed of men who spend their lives studying crime and criminals. In its headquarters are to be found experts from Scotland Yard, many foreign detectives and secret service agents. This book tells of their greatest victories over crime, and is written in association with George Dilnot by a former member of the Criminal Investigation Department of Scotland Yard.

LOOK FOR THE MAN WITH THE GUN

THE DETECTIVE STORY CLUB

FOR DETECTIVE CONNOISSEURS

recommends

"The Man with the Gun."

MR. BALDWIN'S FAVOURITE

THE LEAVENWORTH CASE

By ANNA K. GREEN

THIS exciting detective story, published towards the end of last century, enjoyed an enormous success both in England and America. It seems to have been forgotten for nearly fifty years until Mr. Baldwin, speaking at a dinner of the American Society in London, remarked : " An American woman, a successor of Poe, Anna K. Green, gave us *The Leavenworth Case*, which I still think one of the best detective stories ever written." It is a remarkably clever story, a masterpiece of its kind, and in addition to an exciting murder mystery and the subsequent tracking down of the criminal, the writing and characterisation are excellent. *The Leavenworth Case* will not only grip the attention of the reader from beginning to end but will also be read again and again with increasing pleasure.

CALLED BACK

By HUGH CONWAY

BY the purest of accidents a man who is blind accidentally comes on the scene of a murder. He cannot see what is happening, but he can hear. He is seen by the assassin who, on discovering him to be blind, allows him to go without harming him. Soon afterwards he recovers his sight and falls in love with a mysterious woman who is in some way involved in the crime. . . . The mystery deepens, and only after a series of memorable thrills is the tangled skein unravelled.

LOOK FOR THE MAN WITH THE GUN

THE DETECTIVE STORY CLUB

FOR DETECTIVE CONNOISSEURS

recommends

"The Man with the Gun."

The Murder of Roger Ackroyd

By AGATHA CHRISTIE

THE MURDER OF ROGER ACKROYD is one of Mrs.
Christie's most brilliant detective novels. As a play, under the
title of *Alibi*, it enjoyed a long and successful run with Charles
Laughton as the popular detective, Hercule Poirot. The novel has
now been filmed, and its clever plot, skilful characterisation, and
sparkling dialogue will make every one who sees the film want to
read the book. M. Poirot, the hero of many brilliant pieces of
detective deduction, comes out of his temporary retirement like a
giant refreshed, to undertake the investigation of a peculiarly brutal
and mysterious murder. Geniuses like Sherlock Holmes often find
a use for faithful mediocrities like Dr. Watson, and by a coincidence
it is the local doctor who follows Poirot round and himself tells the
story. Furthermore, what seldom happens in these cases, he is
instrumental in giving Poirot one of the most valuable clues
to the mystery.

LOOK FOR THE MAN WITH THE GUN

THE DETECTIVE STORY CLUB

FOR DETECTIVE CONNOISSEURS

recommends

"The Man with the Gun."

THE PERFECT CRIME

THE FILM STORY OF

ISRAEL ZANGWILL'S famous detective thriller, THE BIG BOW MYSTERY

A MAN is murdered for no apparent reason. He has no enemies, and there seemed to be no motive for any one murdering him. No clues remained, and the instrument with which the murder was committed could not be traced. The door of the room in which the body was discovered was locked and bolted on the inside, both windows were latched, and there was no trace of any intruder. The greatest detectives in the land were puzzled. Here indeed was the perfect crime, the work of a master mind. Can you solve the problem which baffled Scotland Yard for so long, until at last the missing link in the chain of evidence was revealed?

LOOK OUT

FOR FURTHER SELECTIONS FROM THE DETECTIVE STORY CLUB—READY SHORTLY

LOOK FOR THE MAN WITH THE GUN